W9-CHN-822

Jack leaned over and pressed his lips against Shelley's

Shelley kissed him back, thinking it would be so easy to have an affair with him. Then she stepped back, her expression serious. "I'm not playing with you, Jack. It's just that I'm having trouble throwing caution to the wind."

"What are you afraid of? Enjoying it too much?"

Shelley's first inclination was to say no. How could she be afraid of enjoying herself too much? Then she thought about it and admitted the idea made some sense.

It wasn't as if having sex was some kind of monumental event. She was single and free to do what she wanted. So why did she hesitate? Jack Kincaid turned her on. Maybe she *was* afraid of enjoying it too much.

Writing *Flyboy* was truly a labor of love for **Janice Kaiser**. From the time she was six weeks old, she flew with her pilot father in the co-pilot seat of a Cessna 310—the kind of plane hero Jack Kincaid flies in her Temptation novel. Janice had always wanted to write a book about a pilot, and after a wonderful vacation with her husband in the Caribbean, she decided an island paradise would make an ideal romantic setting. And the rest, as they say, is history. Look for Janice Kaiser's miniseries, First Person Personal, coming in the fall of 1993.

Books by Janice Kaiser

HARLEQUIN TEMPTATION
406—HEARTTHROB
417—THE MAVERICK
429—WILDE AT HEART

HARLEQUIN SUPERROMANCE
494—THE BIG SECRET
541—CRADLE OF DREAMS

Don't miss any of our special offers. Write to us at the following address for information on our newest releases.

Harlequin Reader Service
P.O. Box 1397, Buffalo, NY 14240
Canadian address: P.O. Box 603,
Fort Erie, Ont. L2A 5X3

FLYBOY

JANICE KAISER

Harlequin Books

TORONTO • NEW YORK • LONDON
AMSTERDAM • PARIS • SYDNEY • HAMBURG
STOCKHOLM • ATHENS • TOKYO • MILAN
MADRID • WARSAW • BUDAPEST • AUCKLAND

If you purchased this book without a cover you should be aware
that this book is stolen property. It was reported as "unsold and
destroyed" to the publisher, and neither the author nor the
publisher has received any payment for this "stripped book."

For the flyboy's sisters:
Bernice Eleanor Bender,
Elizabeth Bender Duckett
and
Geraldine Bender Peery

Published May 1993

ISBN 0-373-25544-6

FLYBOY

Copyright © 1993 by Belle Lettres, Inc. All rights reserved.
Except for use in any review, the reproduction or utilization
of this work in whole or in part in any form by any electronic,
mechanical or other means, now known or hereafter invented,
including xerography, photocopying and recording, or in any
information storage or retrieval system, is forbidden without
the permission of the publisher, Harlequin Enterprises Limited,
225 Duncan Mill Road, Don Mills, Ontario, Canada M3B 3K9.

All the characters in this book have no existence outside the
imagination of the author and have no relation whatsoever to
anyone bearing the same name or names. They are not even
distantly inspired by any individual known or unknown to the
author, and all incidents are pure invention.

® are Trademarks registered in the United States Patent and
Trademark Office and in other countries.

Printed in U.S.A.

1

JACK KINCAID FELT LIKE hell. His head was throbbing, his eyes felt as though they'd been sandblasted, and his stomach was sour. If it hadn't been for his damn promise, he'd have called the whole thing off. But he was committed to flying Henry Van Dam's niece to Saint Maurice that morning. And like it or not, fly her he would.

Judging from the tone of her letter, he had more than an inkling of what he would face. Shelley Van Dam was determined to settle her uncle's affairs in half the time needed to do a good job. It was clear she'd try to run him ragged—if he let her.

But what could he do? Good old Henry had just died and Jack had agreed to help the niece, so here he was, stretched out on a Naugahyde couch across from Mabel Hooks's desk, instead of in bed.

"You sleepin', honey, or is you just fakin' it?" Mabel asked.

"I'm trying to rest a little before I have to go to work," he muttered without opening his eyes. "Doesn't the safety of the airways count for anything with you?"

"Safety?" she retorted emphatically. "If it was safety you cared about, you'd keep a little more distance between you and ol' demon rum."

Jack Kincaid opened one eye at that remark, annoyed that his integrity was being impugned. He had never particularly cared what people thought about him personally, but he did take a certain pride in his professionalism.

Mabel was looking at him officiously. She was, he reminded himself, secretary to the manager of operations at Harry S. Truman Airport, Charlotte Amalie, Saint Thomas, the U.S. Virgin Islands. That pretty well meant she was in charge.

All in all, Mabel, an enormous woman with an ebony face, was a gem. Still, she wasn't the type to brook nonsense from anybody. At the moment, it was obvious she wasn't too pleased with him.

"If you're goin' to crash that airplane of yours," she said, "I just hopes you do it far from my airport."

Jack lifted his head off the couch. Pain stabbed at the backs of his eyes. "Listen, Mabel, I pay to land here. I don't recall my contract including unsolicited advice."

"Well, I don't recall no contract sayin' you can use my office like a hotel room, either."

He sat up, knowing it was time to cool it. With Mabel Hooks you only went so far, and he'd already passed that point. He ran his fingers through his shaggy brown hair.

"Who's your passenger, anyway?" the secretary asked.

"Her name's Shelley Van Dam."

"A woman! Now, what kind of lady would be so foolish as to pay you to take her flyin'? She don't know nothin' 'bout you, honey, if she done that!" Mabel hooted.

Unfortunately she'd been witness to one of his more embarrassing moments. The young wife of a wealthy client had cornered him in Mabel's office and unabashedly propositioned him, insisting that she could tell that he was as taken with her as she was with him.

In truth, he hadn't been interested in the lady. Kincaid always steered clear of married women. With so many single ones to choose from, he'd figured why complicate things. After all, countless times he'd sworn that his only credo was to do things the easy way.

He pressed his throbbing temples, wishing he had just one more hour of sack time. The morning after, it never seemed worth it, though he did have very pleasant memories of a beauty with an exotic name he'd already forgotten.

"I don't mean to stick my nose in your business none," Mabel said, "but would your passenger be a pretty young lady with more suitcases than the Queen of England?"

Kincaid rolled his head, trying to get the kinks out of his neck. "I haven't any idea what she looks like. My contact with her has been strictly by mail."

"Well, if she is short and blond and pretty, she showed up about twenty minutes ago and she is stomping back and forth outside. She looks fit to be tied."

Kincaid glanced at the clock and moaned. Then he turned and peered out the venetian blinds at a petite blonde dressed in a pale yellow silk blouse, white pants and sandals, who was striding back and forth along a rank of suitcases like a drill sergeant. Every ten seconds or so, she paused, glanced at her watch, flipped her short wavy curls, then resumed pacing.

Kincaid watched her for a moment, then sank back on the couch. He wasn't sure he was up to dealing with that kind of energy, considering his condition.

He rubbed his stubbled chin, wondering if he should have taken the time to shave. On the other hand, he'd always refused to be anyone other than himself, so why start compromising now?

He looked out the window again. Shelley Van Dam was still pacing and examining her watch. Like most people, she'd brought the mainland with her. Thank God he'd left all that behind. Silently, Kincaid cursed the situation. "I don't suppose you'd go out and tell her I crashed on my way up here," he mumbled to Mabel.

"No way, honey. That girl's *your* problem. And if you wants my opinion, you is goin' to have your hands full. You should have seen her when the man done brought her here in the taxicab. Lord, did she have him jumpin'!"

Kincaid took in Henry's niece again, acknowledging that whatever else she was, he couldn't dismiss the fact that she was attractive. Damn attractive! Women were a pain, but a pain he hadn't figured how to live without. So he had limited himself to the ones who were willing to see him on his terms, which tended to be when the mood struck him. That was one reason he relished living on Saint Maurice. Small and relatively unpopulated, it was remote enough to provide the privacy he cherished, but close enough to the larger islands for him to be able to find a party when he wanted one.

But now he had to deal with Shelley Van Dam. And the longer he stalled, the worse it would get. "Mabel, do me a favor and ask Miss Van Dam to come in. I'm going to wash up. I'll be back in a couple of minutes." He went off without waiting for a reply, though as he walked down the hall, he heard Mabel grumbling.

He took longer in the bathroom than he had to, splashing cold water on his face, hoping the puffiness would go away. He dried his face carefully, then, realizing he'd forgotten his comb, ran his fingers through his hair and mustache. He rubbed his grizzled chin, and with a shrug, returned to the office. He found Shelley standing in the middle of the room, her arms folded over her breasts, her green eyes flashing.

"Mr. Kincaid, do you realize I've been waiting nearly twenty minutes for you? I admit this isn't New York, or for that matter Los Angeles, but aren't you overdoing the laid-back routine a little?"

Jack stepped toward her, his hand extended. "You must be Henry's niece. It's so nice to meet you, Miss Van Dam," he said, his voice full of false affability.

Shelley took his hand, flushing as she realized that she was being chastised for her rudeness. "Sorry if I sounded curt," she murmured. "I have an aversion to inefficiency."

"That's all right," he replied. "We're used to it. Aren't we, Mabel?"

"Speak for youself," Mabel replied. "I don't have no trouble with nobody. Except maybe you, sometimes. And I never is late."

The remark brought Jack up short. He glanced at Shelley, who laughed.

"Sounds like you have a reputation," she said.

He looked her in the eye, annoyed that she was so amused by Mabel's put-down. For a moment they stared at each other. The spark in her eye told him she wasn't going to be intimidated by anything he said or did. Kincaid couldn't let her stare him down, so he didn't.

A slight smile touched Shelley's lips before she finally looked away. His gaze went to her sensuous mouth. Her lips were generous, inviting even. He liked what he saw, though he wasn't so keen on what he'd heard.

"Tell you what," Shelley said, with an unmistakable air of confidence, "you gather yourself, and I'll wait out front. But please don't take long. I hate to waste time." With that, she turned and went out the door.

Kincaid watched her go, his eyes drifting down her shapely figure. There was a sauciness about her that was as cute as it was hostile. When she'd gone, he turned to Mabel.

"Don't bother sayin' nothin' to me, Jackie," she said. "I is too busy to hear it."

"What I ought to do is take my business elsewhere," he muttered.

"Like where you thinkin', honey? Cuba, maybe?"

Jack gave her a tight smile. "I'd get a friendlier welcome, that's for sure." He moved toward the window for a better look at Shelley Van Dam. It was hard to tell which was stronger, his resistance to her assertive manner or his fascination with it. "She's a firecracker, Mabel. At the moment, I just can't tell if that's good or bad." He looked back at the secretary.

"Oh, you'll find out soon enough." Mabel's smile turned devilish. "I'll be prayin' for you, honey. Somethin' tells me you'll need it."

A COUPLE OF MINUTES later, Shelley turned at the sound of his footsteps. At the rate they were going she figured they would need at least a month to get everything accomplished. But she had dealt with enough difficult people for too many years to let that get her down. So she put a smile on her lips and resolved to be firm. Experience had taught her that often did the trick.

He gestured toward the line of suitcases. "Do you have an entourage, Miss Van Dam, or are you of the school that believes every airplane needs extra ballast?"

"Mr. Kincaid," she began, "I know you probably consider me pushy and unpleasant, but I simply have to do things my way. I'm taking time out of a very busy schedule to tend to Uncle Henry's affairs because it's something that has to be done. This is not a vacation for me."

Kincaid studied her. "Did I say something I shouldn't have?"

She sighed. "I don't mean to lecture, but I know from what Uncle Henry told me that you tend to want to do things your own way."

"Plainly, you do, too."

"Yes, well, that's true. But I happen to be the one paying the bill."

"Look," he said with annoyance, "if this is going to degenerate into a labor dispute, I can settle things real fast. I don't need your money. The only reason I'm here is because of Henry. I sort of feel an obligation. On the other hand, I stopped jumping through hoops a long time ago."

Shelley Van Dam calmly considered her options. Kincaid could make her job a lot easier—if he was willing to cooperate. If he wouldn't, she might be better off dealing with another charter pilot. "Maybe our differences are irreconcilable, Mr. Kincaid. Maybe this just isn't going to work out."

"Maybe not."

"Despite some of the things Uncle Henry said about you, I thought the fact that you knew him would be helpful. My uncle insisted that you could be trusted, and that's important to me. I value trustworthiness."

"Presumably Henry also mentioned I wasn't very obedient," Kincaid replied. "If he didn't, he should have."

Unhappy with the direction of the conversation, Shelley fell silent.

"Look," he said, "I'd make it easy on us both and tell you to find yourself another pilot, but I'll be honest with you. If you want to fly into Saint Maurice, I'm it. Your only other option is to charter a boat. I can give you some names if that's what you'd like to do."

Shelley put her hands on her hips. "What do you mean, you're it?"

"No one else will land an airplane on Saint Maurice." He gave her a half smile. "Well, maybe I shouldn't say no one. You can always find a daredevil who'll do anything for a buck. But it might take you a few days to locate one."

"You're joking, of course."

"No ma'am. The strip's private, uncontrolled and dangerous. To a pilot, it's sort of like trying to land on somebody's driveway."

"You're saying that you're the one with the upper hand. Isn't that the point?"

"I'm saying that I work under my own terms."

"That's exactly what I mean." Frustrated by his smugness, she turned and stared across the field. A single-engine private plane was touching down on the far runway. "All right," she finally said. "The bottom line is, if we work together, we do things your way."

"Something like that."

"Will you at least do me the courtesy of telling me exactly what that entails?"

He smiled. "It's pretty simple, really. I don't like being ordered around like a shavetail second lieutenant. You want to go someplace, tell me and I'll get you there. You want to talk to somebody, I'll arrange it. Don't tell me how to do my job, Miss Van Dam, and I won't tell you how to do yours."

She slowly nodded. "I take it you were once a shavetail second lieutenant, as you put it, and didn't much care for it."

"Yes. And I was once somebody's husband. And that somebody had a whole lifelong agenda for me. That was when I discovered I wanted to do things my own way—either that, or not bother doing them at all."

"I'm beginning to understand you, Mr. Kincaid," Shelley replied.

He glanced up at the sun. "It's starting to get warm and you probably don't want to stand around here any more than I do. What'll it be, Miss Van Dam? Are you coming with me, or do I fly home alone?"

"I want to go to Saint Maurice and see the plantation house. Since I don't have the time to go by boat, I guess that means I'm going with you."

"Fine. The first step, then, is the boarding process." He took his aviator glasses from his shirt pocket and slipped them on. Then he pointed at the suitcases. "This is really all yours?"

"Yes. Is that going to be a problem?"

"Only for whoever has to carry it." He gave her a crooked grin, his gaze resting an extra moment on her breasts.

Shelley groaned. The last thing she needed was for some flyboy Romeo to start getting ideas.

"So who carries my luggage? You or me?"

"The job calls for an expert," he said. "I'll get a porter and you wait here and relax." With that he walked off, leaving her standing on the sidewalk.

Why was she so surprised by Jack Kincaid? Her uncle had warned her that the pilot was laid-back to the point of lethargic, and bullheaded to boot—all said with admiration, because Henry Van Dam had been a lot that way himself.

The flesh-and-blood Jack Kincaid wasn't a lot different from the mental picture of him she'd created. The tousled brown hair and thick mustache, both in need of a trim, the day's growth of beard and pale-blue bloodshot eyes were all in keeping with the image. He was complacent, self-satisfied and didn't seem to give a tinker's damn what the world thought of him.

But she hadn't foreseen him being quite so clever. He had managed to get the upper hand, and rather easily, too. That most definitely didn't bode well for the future. The last thing she needed was to be deterred from the business at hand. She had earmarked ten days to handle Uncle

Henry's estate. When that time was up, she would return to the States.

She checked her watch as a big jet came gliding down over the hilltop and settled on the runway a few hundred yards from where she was standing. She looked around for Kincaid and spotted him fifty yards away, making his way back along the tarmac with a porter in tow. The man was pushing a dolly, his dusky brow shining with perspiration. Jack was joking with him and they were both laughing as though they had all day.

At one point they came to a stop so the porter could light a cigarette. An animated and stationary conversation ensued. The harder Shelley stared, the longer they seemed to linger. She closed her eyes and told herself to calm down and not let the guy get to her. If she let him know how much he annoyed her, much less complained about it, he'd undoubtedly get worse.

The two men finally started ambling her way again and she put a smile on her face. Watching Kincaid, she couldn't help thinking he was rubbing it in, exaggerating his nonchalance to make a point. But she refused to let her pique show, even though her smile felt as though it was about to crack.

Shelley looked Jack Kincaid over. It was hard not to. She guessed him to be in his mid-thirties. He was tall—probably six-one or -two—and sinewy. In fact there was a certain elegance about him. Too bad he annoyed her so damned much.

He wore a faded khaki short-sleeved shirt, khaki trousers and dark-brown deck shoes. His yellow aviator glasses were pushed up into his thick hair. A couple of pens and what looked like a small notebook were protruding from the breast pocket of his shirt.

As he drew near, there was a hint of amusement on his face. He sort of looked her over, though ostensibly he was listening to the porter's animated speech. She felt a sexual awareness—a man-woman thing that inevitably surfaced between the sexes at one point or another. Shelley managed to sustain her smile.

"Hope you didn't get too hot standing out in the sun," he said affably.

"Oh, no, I love the heat. Anyway, somebody had to guard the luggage."

He smiled as stiffly as she. "Never can be too careful."

She looked into his bloodshot eyes and beamed. "All ready, are we?"

Jack gestured for the porter to load up. The man promptly began putting her bags on the dolly. They watched the loading process. "You don't believe in traveling light, do you?" he remarked.

"No. No, I don't."

They exchanged wooden smiles.

There were just a few bags left. Kincaid stepped over and picked one up, having to hitch his back because of the unexpected weight. "Good Lord, what's in here? Your stereo system?"

"No, that one is filled with Uncle Henry's journals."

He looked at her quizzically. "The ones he sent you a couple of months ago?"

"Yes. You know about that?"

"I was the one who mailed them for him. Ol' Henry was very anxious to get them off the island and into safe hands. I'm not so sure it's such a good idea to be bringing them back."

"Why not?"

"I don't know why, but he seemed to think it was important that they not be around."

Shelley was aware of Henry's anxiety about the notebooks, but hadn't taken it very seriously. He'd had numerous odd quirks and she had considered the business about the notebooks just another one.

Henry Van Dam had been an eccentric, a kind of mad scientist, to put it mildly. Her mother had insisted the old boy was nuts, but Shelley hadn't wanted to judge him quite so harshly. In fact, she'd always felt a real fondness for her father's unusual brother.

One of her most cherished memories was the trip her family had made to Saint Maurice when she was twelve. The tiny island in the French group had been virtually untouched by civilization. She remembered the unrelenting heat, the mosquitoes and lizards, and Uncle Henry's wonderful old plantation house that belonged in a Graham Greene novel.

His work and all his strange ideas about medicine had seemed most fascinating. She'd experienced the benefit of one of his cures firsthand when some insect bites she'd gotten became infected. Henry had concocted an herbal lotion he'd obtained from a tribal medicine man in Guatemala. It had stopped the itching and healed the inflammation.

However, what stood out most in Shelley's memory was the sight of a large glass container full of insects in Uncle Henry's laboratory. When she asked what they were, her uncle had told her they were soldier termites he'd brought back from the Central African Republic for study. He'd seen a native healer wash and crush them to use as a poultice on a man suffering from a subcutaneous amoebic infection that the Western doctors hadn't been able to cure.

Shelley had been thrilled by his tales of medicine men and their esoteric remedies. Still, she had seen her uncle rarely. Their last contact had been two years earlier, when they both happened to be in New York at the same time—Henry to conduct some of his mysterious business concerning pharmaceuticals, Shelley to meet with the heads of various charities in the arts.

They'd met in the lobby of The Pierre, Henry in a rumpled white suit and floppy bow tie, looking like some kind of exotic bird imprisoned in a zoo, his eyes darting around as though other people were wild animals, not fellow members of his own species.

"I'm getting along in years, Shelley," he'd told her, "and when I go, I guess everything I have will go to you."

"Mom and Dad provided well for me, Uncle Henry," she'd told him. "If you wish to give your things to a research facility or something, I would certainly understand."

"It's not the value of the tangible assets that's at issue. I'm sure you'd want to sell the plantation house. I'm more concerned about my research. There's a wealth of information in my head that I wouldn't want to see fall into the wrong hands."

"What wrong hands?"

"All of them," he'd said, vaguely waving at their surroundings—at what she assumed him to mean the civilized world.

At the time, she'd dismissed what Henry had said as a product of his eccentric nature—his "paranoia," as her mother had called it. Then, later, she'd received a box full of Henry's notebooks. In his careful, cramped handwriting were pages and pages of observations about folk cures and exotic plants. The enclosed letter implied their value was immense. "Centuries of knowledge is in my research, most of it unrecorded anywhere else," he'd written. "There are 250,000 species of plants in the world, and scientists have studied little more than a thousand of them. Probably 40,000 contain substances with undiscovered medicinal and nutritional value. A lifetime of work, Shelley, and I've barely scratched the surface."

She was impressed, but what was she to do with the notebooks? In a postscript, Henry had added that if anything should happen to him, she'd be given instructions. When word of her uncle's death had reached her, she'd become truly concerned.

She had called the departmental authorities in Guadeloupe to learn what she could about the circumstances of his death. The French doctor who'd come over from Saint Barthelemy said the old man had died after a fall down the stairs. An inquest had been undertaken and the results were pending. In his letter, Jack Kincaid had said that the police had sealed the plantation house. Shelley's biggest task would be to work out the legal matters with Uncle Henry's attorney, and to dispose of the property.

She'd assumed the instructions regarding the notebooks would either be with the attorney, or among her uncle's effects. Since she'd expected to dispose of everything, it had made sense to cart them along with her. However, Jack Kincaid's reaction made her wonder if she hadn't made a mistake.

They were walking toward the plane, which was parked some distance away on the tarmac. The porter was following behind, pushing the dolly. Shelley glanced over at Jack.

"Do you think it was stupid to bring Uncle Henry's notebooks along?" she asked.

"I don't know," he answered with a shrug. "Henry didn't confide in me much, so I really can't judge. Our friendship didn't involve his work, except to the extent that I flew him around on his various expeditions. He seemed to like it that way."

"What sort of friendship did you have, if you don't mind me asking?"

"We were the only two English-speaking people on the island. Even so, after I arrived, it was months before we had a real conversation. Chess initially drew us together. We both played and started getting together regularly, usually on Sunday afternoons. My airplane was also a factor. The man I bought it from, Jean Favre, had flown Henry around. Following Jean's death, Henry began chartering planes out of Saint Barts, but it was just too inconvenient. About the time we began playing chess, Henry inquired about my services. The rest, as they say, is history."

"You knew nothing about Uncle Henry's work?"

"No. He made a point of not talking about it."

They reached the Cessna 310. Kincaid opened the cargo door and the porter began loading Shelley's luggage. She watched Jack carefully, trying to assess how credible he was, and whether she believed he was telling her everything.

"Mr. Kincaid, did you have the impression that my uncle was in some sort of danger these last months?"

He gave her a thoughtful look, but didn't seem as surprised by the question as she would have expected. "Henry was an unusual man with unusual attitudes toward people. It wasn't easy to tell what he was thinking."

"You're evading my question."

He looked as if he was mildly amused by her probing. "I believe Henry thought he had a problem of some sort."

Jack Kincaid's reticence struck her as curious. "What sort of problem?"

"I don't know."

"You don't know, or you don't want to say?"

"Your uncle was never very specific—let me put it that way."

"He didn't explain why he was sending me the journals?"

"He wanted them safe, like I told you."

Shelley started feeling a bit more suspicious. "Didn't that make you curious, Mr. Kincaid?"

"It's Jack, by the way. If we're going to play grand inquisitor, we might as well be familiar."

"All right," she agreed, ignoring the sarcasm. "I'm Shelley. But please, be straight with me. I want to learn everything I can about what was going on in Uncle Henry's life."

"I don't know if I can be of much help," he said with a level look.

"Do you have any idea at all what he was afraid of?"

He sighed impatiently. "Look, Shelley. Henry was a strange old bird—I don't have to tell you that. He was looking over his shoulder from the day I met him. I tried not to pry into his business, and he didn't volunteer much. About all I know for sure is that he was researching folk cures. What he was trying to achieve, I have no idea."

"You said Uncle Henry had some sort of problem. That he was always looking over his shoulder. Isn't there anything more specific you can tell me?"

The porter had long since finished loading the luggage and was sitting on his dolly, mopping his brow. Jack took out his wallet and handed the man a five-dollar bill. Thanking them both, the porter trudged off, pushing the dolly. Jack watched him for a moment, then turned back to Shelley, who was waiting for his answer.

"I'm reluctant even to mention this," he said, "but over the last year or so Henry had been acting more paranoid than usual. He gave me the impression he was afraid of something—somebody who was out to get either him or his research. A few weeks before he died, he asked me to alert him if any strangers showed up on the island. He said he was expecting trouble. When I asked what kind of trouble, he said his very existence was regarded by some people to be a threat. But he wouldn't elaborate."

"That's fairly specific."

"Yeah, but what does it mean?" Jack asked.

"Somebody was after him. That was why he sent me his journals."

He nodded. "Yes, but Henry's gone now and the puzzle's died with him. It's even possible he was imagining the whole thing. With Henry, it was hard to know."

Shelley looked him over. Was he telling her the whole story? One minute Jack acted concerned that she'd brought the journals back with her, the next he was dismissing the whole thing as a product of her uncle's paranoia. Perhaps she'd been unwise to assume that her uncle knew what he was talking about when he'd written her that Jack Kincaid was a man to be trusted. "It's kind of coincidental that Uncle Henry happened to die now, isn't it?"

"Why ask me?" he returned.

She stared into his bloodshot eyes. "Do you think Henry's death was an accident?"

"That's what people say, Shelley, but I really have no way of knowing."

She folded her arms and they looked at each other, neither giving ground. "Why do I have a feeling you're playing games with me, Jack?"

"Maybe because we don't operate the same way," he replied smoothly. "Or maybe you just don't want to trust me," he added with a smile.

When Shelley didn't respond he closed the door of the cargo compartment. Then he pulled his aviator glasses down so they shielded his eyes. "Guess it's time to get rolling. Air Saint Maurice's flight number one now boarding at gate one. Please have your boarding pass ready."

"Do you serve the drinks on board, too?" she asked wryly.

"If you want booze on my plane, honey, you'll have to bring your own. The pilot, being the conscientious type, restricts his personal libation to the night before."

"So one would hope."

Jack Kincaid grinned. Then he climbed up the starboard wing of the craft and unlocked the cockpit door. Coming back for her, he offered his hand and lifted her right up onto the wing, grabbing her waist to steady her.

Shelley looked up into his eyes as she noticed the warmth of his hand against her body. Before she could even think about pulling away from him, he let go of her waist. Then, guiding her safely into the copilot's seat, he said, "I'll need a minute or so to check everything out. Wouldn't want to take you up in something that doesn't belong in the air."

Shelley could feel the blood drain from her face at his comment. He winked in response to her distressed look, then climbed back down to the ground. She could tell that the man was pleased with himself, and perhaps a touch too self-assured for her taste. Shelley decided to ignore his come-on. At this moment, all she cared about was whether or not he could fly.

2

IT WAS SWELTERING IN the cabin of the plane. Shelley tried to relax, knowing they would soon be airborne, but it wasn't easy for her. She hated having things rest entirely in someone else's hands.

She watched Kincaid moving around the aircraft, inspecting the props and the landing gear. It was difficult to tell if he was putting on a show, or if he was a lot more professional than he looked. One thing was for sure—he was moving with more efficiency than she would have expected.

He drained the gas-tank sumps and checked for water in the fuselage. She found this new side of him appealing. True, she would have felt better if he were clean-shaven, and if his eyes didn't look quite so bleary. But in spite of everything, Jack Kincaid had a reassuring manner about him, even if, as a man, he confounded her.

As he turned the props, she noticed how strong his arms and shoulders looked as they strained the fabric of his shirt. And the grin under his mustached lip, the gleam of the aviator glasses in the sun, contributed to his aura of cool efficiency.

He finally climbed into the cockpit, slipped past her to get into the pilot's seat and pulled the door closed behind him.

"Hot yet?" he asked.

Shelley realized she was perspiring. "To put it mildly."

"Sorry, but I'm going to have to add to your misery. We'll have to cinch you up like turkey trussed for the oven."

"What a wonderful metaphor."

He helped her with her seat belt, giving it a firm tug to secure her.

"I take it there's no air-conditioning," she said, dabbing her brow with a tissue from her purse.

"Just God's natural cooling that comes with altitude. It'll be a lot more comfortable once we get airborne. If you're really suffering, we can open the door." He reached across her, his arm lightly grazing her breast as he released the latch and pushed the door open. "You'll have to hang on to the handle while we taxi. And ignore the rattle—it won't affect how she flies."

She watched, fascinated, as he seemed to go through some kind of preflight checklist. Then he flipped the ignition switches and fired the engine on his side of the plane. Once it had smoothed out, he asked if everything was clear on her side. Seeing no one around, Shelley told him it was. He fired the starboard engine.

Now that they were about to take off, Shelley felt a surge of excitement. But she was nervous, too. When she looked over at Jack, he winked reassuringly. She smiled, realizing that for the first time that day things weren't strained between them. Yet in an odd way, the friendliness seemed appropriate to their present circumstances.

The air coming in the open door was refreshing, and Shelley started feeling better. She listened to Jack talk to the tower, but she couldn't distinguish a word he said over the noise of the engines. When the plane began moving, she hung on to the door.

After they got to the end of the taxiway, they waited for a commercial jet that was making its descent toward the field. Jack reached over and closed the cockpit door. "Time to button up," he said.

The big jet glided down in front of them, sending up puffs of smoke when the wheels touched the runway. Jack got on the radio again, talking to the tower.

"Here we go," he said, taking a final glance at the sky before pulling the Cessna out onto the concrete strip.

The engines roared and as they raced along, the craft shook like a car badly in need of new shocks. But then they lifted into the air and the feel of the plane turned sweet. They banked to the south, circling back over Lindbergh Bay.

Shelley could see the yachts sprinkled over the water and a small cruise ship entering the port. A seaplane glided in for a landing, kicking up a wake in the aqua waters of the bay. It was already cooler in the cabin, the temperature dropping steadily as they ascended.

Far out on the horizon to the south she could see Saint Croix, and the more rugged profile of Saint John ahead. Smaller islands dotted the seascape. Jack Kincaid began leveling off. He moved the earphone nearest her forward on his cheek and looked at her.

"Feel better?"

"Yes, much."

He glanced down at her body, looking like he was about to make some sort of salacious remark. But then he said, "If that belt's too constricting, you can loosen it now."

She immediately began trying to ease it, though without much success.

"I'm afraid the equipment's a little worse for wear," he said apologetically. "Here, let me help." He slid his fingers under the belt and across the soft flesh of her abdomen until he had the clamp loosened. His hand didn't linger unnecessarily, and she couldn't say the touch was

inappropriate, but there was an obvious sexual awareness on both their parts. Shelley tried to ignore it. Even so,
a vague sense of uneasiness went through her.

As Jack Kincaid focused his attention on the instru-
ments, she tried to put the incident out of her mind. But
no matter how hard she tried, she couldn't forget that she
was headed for an isolated island with a man who was
unlike anyone she'd ever known.

Shelley had always felt she could handle any situation
that came up. However, Jack Kincaid presented a different kind of challenge, though she wasn't entirely sure what
it was. In any case, it wasn't worth worrying about, considering she wouldn't be around him for long. In a week
or so, Uncle Henry's estate should be settled and she would
be returning home.

Shelley studied Jack, who was writing in his small
notebook, seemingly oblivious to her.

She noted the slight bump in the middle of his nose, and
his strong jaw. He was, after all, a sort of vagabond. It
didn't seem to bother Jack Kincaid that his hair was
mussed, and his chin stubbled, or that his shirt was wrinkled and sweat-stained. That was the way he lived. His
very manner left little doubt about that. Nevertheless she
still found him terribly sexy.

She couldn't recall a man affecting her quite this way—
not in the three years since her divorce, anyway. Which
was not to say she didn't come into contact with appealing men. In fact, she dated a lot, though mostly in pro
forma fashion. So many of the guys she went out with were
simply boys in men's bodies—even the more sophisticated ones. Her relationships were, more often than not,
less than satisfying. De rigueur sex was a real turnoff. For
that reason, men with less libido were definitely more en-
joyable companions.

At least Warren Dixon, the entertainment lawyer she'd been dating the past six months, had his priorities straight and his feet on the ground. He was levelheaded, organized, and he wasn't into the usual games. They thought alike and she found comfort in that. The subject of marriage had come up obliquely, but neither she nor Warren was in a hurry.

And that was precisely what made the sexual attraction she was beginning to feel for Jack Kincaid so unnerving. Being affected by a man's raw animal magnetism was most unexpected. Not to mention the fact that Jack was probably the least likely candidate on earth for an involvement.

Still, she would keep her guard up. He didn't seem the type who'd let his opportunities slip by untested. At some point he'd make a pass at her. She wondered what his line would be. He'd probably try something pretty direct—a simple question, such as "How about going to my place for a drink?" Shelley smiled to herself as she tried to picture how he'd be at taking rejection. One thing for sure—with her, he'd never get to first base.

THE NEXT THING SHELLEY knew, Jack Kincaid was shaking her arm, trying to wake her up. "We'll be landing soon," he said over the sound of the engines. "It's not a good idea to be asleep when we touch down."

Shelley rubbed her eyes, amazed that she'd slept so soundly, considering the relative discomfort of the aircraft.

She sat up straight, then glanced out the windshield. Several miles ahead an island the shape of a kidney bean rose from the emerald and aqua waters of the Caribbean. There was a single high point in the center—more a large hill than a mountain—surrounded by a low plain covered with dense vegetation.

They were headed toward a crescent-shaped bay on the leeward side of the island. It was ringed by a white sandy beach and a line of feathery palms. A cluster of buildings was half hidden in the trees, their metal roofs shining in the sun.

When Shelley had come to Saint Maurice as a child, her family had arrived by the yacht her father had chartered. They had anchored in the bay and rowed ashore in a small boat. Uncle Henry had been on the beach to greet them in his rumpled white suit and shaggy hair, his battered Panama hat in his big, bony hand. Shelley had propped herself on the bow as they approached the beach and watched him waving at them with his hat, a sort of latter-day Robinson Crusoe welcoming them to paradise.

There being no roads or vehicles, their suitcases had been loaded on a donkey that Uncle Henry's servant, a withered Frenchman named Girard, allowed Shelley to lead along the jungle trail to the plantation house. Even at twelve, she had appreciated how special the experience was—a journey back in time. From what Henry had written her since that visit, not a great deal had changed.

"Where's the airport?" Shelley asked, not spotting a landing strip anywhere.

Jack laughed. "The 'airport,' as you call it, is a rather modest stretch of asphalt and gravel to the left of the mountain. You'll see it in a moment."

"Then there's no real airfield? You weren't kidding about that driveway business?"

"Honey, you're sitting in the only plane that regularly uses it. There's not even a windsock. I judge the wind by the surf and the laundry on the clotheslines."

Shelley experienced a sick feeling as the weight of his words struck home. Saint Maurice was not a place bathed in nostalgia, it was a place posing considerable problems.

"Are you saying that to make me nervous?" she asked, swallowing hard.

"No, it's all true. Don't worry. I've landed here a hundred times and haven't crashed yet. Once I even landed in the dead of night with nothing to guide me in but the headlights of the island Jeep and a couple of people with flashlights."

"Please don't tell me you do this for thrills, Kincaid."

"No, I do it because I'm the only one who can." He grinned at her. "Never did like crowds."

They were very close to the island and less than five hundred feet above the water. As they came nearer, Jack banked the plane sharply over the tiny village.

"I'm buzzing to let Chantal know we're here," he explained.

"Who's Chantal?"

"She's sort of the mayor. She'll bring the Jeep out to the strip. Except for a few motorbikes, there's only one vehicle on the island and we all share it. Otherwise we'd have to lug your suitcases half a mile through the jungle to get to Henry's place."

"How quaint," she replied, over the sound of the engine.

"Simple conditions are a great equalizer, my dear. And I'm afraid even a fat checkbook won't bring a limo out to greet you."

"I'm not the snob you seem to think I am, Jack."

"I wasn't suggesting you were. It's just that some people are a lot more dependent on civilization than they're willing to admit. I was trying to point out that on Saint Maurice, a person's got to make do."

"You worry about landing the plane," she shot back. "I'll worry about me."

He touched his brow in a sort of mock salute, grinning all the while. They had circled back out over the sea and were headed toward land again, although from a different angle than before. Ahead Shelley could see a strip cut in the jungle, looking more like a tiny stretch of road than a true runway.

She gripped her seat as the plane descended and settled smoothly onto the runway. Jack braked abruptly then, and they came to a halt a couple of hundred feet from the trees at the far end of the strip.

He glanced over at her. "Doing it by flashlight's even more of a thrill," he said nonchalantly. "If you feel like some night flying."

"I've had plenty of excitement already, thanks."

Jack shook his head. "City girls."

Shelley laughed. The guy certainly liked to strut. But she was glad he knew how to fly the plane.

Kincaid taxied over to the corrugated-steel roof with the four supporting columns that served as a hangar. Pulling right in, he killed the engines and said, "Welcome to Saint Maurice."

She stretched in her seat. "Thank you for making it without crashing."

He was fiddling with the switches on the control panel. "You didn't doubt me, did you?"

"City girls are skeptics by nature, Jack. I would have thought you knew that."

He gave her a bemused look, reached across her and opened the door. She struggled with her seat belt for a moment, before finally getting the thing unlatched.

"Your plane needs maintenance," she said.

"True, but if you think this is bad, wait till you see Henry's place." He unfastened his seat belt and put his hand on the back of her seat. "If you don't mind some friendly advice, Shelley, learn to go with the flow while you're here, or you're going to drive yourself batty."

"I don't expect to be around long enough to go batty. But if you'll get me where I need to go in a timely fashion, I'm sure I can keep my frustrations to a minimum."

"I'll do my best," he replied, smiling.

He gestured for her to disembark. Shelley grabbed her purse, then climbed out and down the wing, without waiting for him. The first thing she noticed was the rich, verdant odor of the jungle—the smell immediately evoking memories of her earlier visit. Uncle Henry had taken her on walks through the island's lush vegetation, naming virtually every specimen of flora and fauna they came across. But foremost, she had been struck by the sense of utter isolation. They could have been in the middle of the Amazon.

She turned as Jack clambered down, landing heavily beside her. It was hot, and there were beads of perspiration on his forehead. She suddenly became conscious of how sticky she was. Her blouse was clinging to her skin. "I'm certainly looking forward to a shower," she said.

"Let's hope there's enough water in the cistern for one."

She scoffed. "Uncle Henry had running water, even when I was here as a child."

"The place is run-down now, Shelley. Things don't work as they should."

She stared at him. Was this another one of his subtle swipes at her inability to cope? She decided to let it pass without comment.

"Since you're such an illustrious visitor, we'll forgo passport formalities," he teased. "Truth is, we had a customs stamp once, but it's been lost for a couple of years now."

"My, things on Saint Maurice *are* primitive. I'm beginning to see what you mean."

He removed his aviator glasses and stuffed them in his pocket. "Well, I guess I'd better unload the baggage. No porters here."

"I'll help."

"No, you just make yourself at home. There'll be a charge for donkey work in your bill." He opened the cargo compartment and set to work unloading the luggage.

Shelley looked around. The undergrowth across the road was dense. There were broad-leaved plants that looked like banana trees, though she could see no fruit. Vines hung from the canopy overhead and an occasional bird could be seen darting through the lush foliage.

Perhaps because of her experience on the island as a child, she always associated the jungle with loneliness. And despite her uncle's seeming contentment with his life, she'd assumed that fundamentally he'd been lonely and unfulfilled. Her mother had assured her that Henry lived that way out of choice, but Shelley couldn't understand it. Even now, it was difficult to fathom. What made a man choose such a life?

It was too late to ask Uncle Henry, but Jack Kincaid wasn't all that different, and he seemed to have known her uncle a lot better than she had. She turned as he dropped the last of her suitcases at the end of the long line he'd formed in the dust. He was perspiring heavily from the exertion.

"At a time like this, don't you hunger for a little civilization?" she asked.

"You mean an airport jammed with people, cars and buses spewing fumes, horns honking and everybody shoving one another to get to the head of a line?"

"Yes, and porters to carry your luggage, and air-conditioned limos to take you to your hotel where a hot shower is waiting."

"You should have stayed in Los Angeles, Shelley."

She sat down on one of the larger suitcases. "Well, I didn't, Jack, and we both know why. Why are *you* here?"

"The easy answer is I don't like people underfoot. But it's more than that. When you live in a beautiful, isolated place like this, you find out who you are. And you either learn to accept yourself, or you don't."

It was pretty obvious that whatever Jack had found out about himself, he was at peace with himself. His air of self-acceptance told her that.

Shelley watched him lean against the wing of the Cessna, his arms folded over his chest. He was looking at her with the roguish grin that seemed to be his trademark. Jack struck her as extremely provocative just then, standing casually with one leg crossed over the other, his tanned flesh gleaming with perspiration, his blue eyes joyously defiant.

"I didn't mean to pry," she said, suddenly feeling self-conscious about how affected she was by his presence. "I was just curious why you came here."

"I don't mind talking about it." He ran his fingers back through his damp hair. "I guess you can give my ex credit for it."

"Your ex-wife?"

"Yeah."

"You're saying she didn't like your independent ways?"

"Let's say she had my life laid out for me—job, home, bank account, money. Especially money. Beth knew exactly what she wanted and organized my life accordingly. She'd decided I was going to be a captain for a commercial airline, bring in six figures, buy her a big gaudy house, a vacation home, a country-club membership, and things—lots of *things*."

He paused to watch a tiny lizard scamper across the dusty ground and disappear into the undergrowth. "Of course, she had her virtues, too. Beth was a doer. She had a lot of energy and was always on the go—sort of like you in that respect—on top of everything, and thoroughly impatient with those less driven."

She rolled her eyes. "Well, that certainly explains a lot! No wonder you haven't been too enthusiastic about working for me."

He chuckled. "Don't worry. I can handle almost anything in small doses. Anyway, the similarities between you and Beth are limited."

"How can you be so presumptuous as to think you know what I'm like?" she huffed. "We only met this morning."

He shrugged. "You could be right. My judgment of women is obviously fallible, so maybe I shouldn't have said anything."

"You might be a capable pilot, Mr. Kincaid, but a diplomat you are not." Then she got up and strolled the short distance to the road, which wasn't much more than a double-rutted trail. "Where's our ride?"

"The Jeep might have been tied up with something else. Or Chantal may not have heard us buzz the village. If she doesn't show up in fifteen or twenty minutes, I'll go find her."

Shelley tried to accept his laid-back attitude, but she was itching to get going. "I guess in all this jungle, smoke signals would be useless."

"I'll look for her now, if it'll make you happy."

There was an edge in his voice, prompting her to raise her hands in surrender. "Oh, no, I'm not supposed to tell you your business. That was our deal. I'll just wait until you're good and ready."

If Jack caught the sarcasm, he showed no sign of it. To hide her impatience, she casually strolled onto the landing strip. The cloudless sky gave a feeling of openness in contrast to the closeness of the jungle. She looked back at Jack. He was still leaning against the wing of his plane, watching her.

Shelley walked a bit one way, then the other, taking measured strides, trying to act as if it really didn't matter whether or not a simple airport transfer took all day. She was aware of Jack Kincaid's eyes on her, his unrelenting self-satisfied smile, and she began wondering if a woman who reminded a guy of his ex-wife would be a turn-on or a real downer. Would he attempt to seduce her out of spite, or would he be repulsed by the mere thought?

After a while, she made her way back to the plane and sat down on a suitcase. She sighed and looked at Jack. He still hadn't moved, but he continued to stare at her, making her increasingly uncomfortable. "So, what did your wife look like?" she asked.

A grin creased the corners of his mouth. "She was a tall brunette with bedroom eyes and loose morals."

Shelley looked down with embarrassment. "I think I'll let that one pass."

He laughed. "Tell me, why haven't you married? Is there something in the Van Dam gene pool that keeps you feisty and independent like ol' Henry was?"

"As a matter of fact, I'm divorced, the same as you."

"God, don't tell me the guy was an irascible pilot."

"Hardly. You and Trent have virtually nothing in common."

"That's a relief."

"What difference does it make? I didn't come here to marry you. In fact, I'll be grateful if you can keep this job I've got from stretching into next year. I'm beginning to get the feeling that planning to get everything done in a week or so was overly optimistic."

"So what did Trent do?" he asked, brushing aside her effort to divert the conversation.

Shelley crossed her legs. "You're going to make me tell you, aren't you?"

"I'm not going to twist your arm."

She knew she didn't have to say anything. She owed Jack Kincaid absolutely nothing. But by the same token this feeling-out process was probably a good way to reduce the tension between them. When people knew each other it was easier to relax and stick to business. "Trent was rich. Very rich."

"What's wrong with that? You don't strike me as a socialist."

"I'm not. My family was pretty well-off, so Trent's wealth didn't change my life. His attitude was the problem. To put it bluntly, he was self-indulgent, selfish, self-centered and didn't have an industrious bone in his body. I think it was the last that bothered me most."

"In other words, being rich is fine, but being idle rich isn't."

"Being *idle* isn't."

"Are you saying that anyone without a regular job is some kind of parasite?"

She could see she'd touched a nerve. "Not at all. But there's so much that needs doing in this world, I think everyone should assume their fair share—at least to the level of their capability."

"And how do you contribute, Shelley?"

"I run the charitable trust my father set up before his death. In recent years, the corpus has become substantial. I'm responsible for many millions of dollars earmarked annually for charitable purposes."

"Such as?"

"We've targeted a few areas where we think we can make a difference. One is supporting creative persons in the arts, another is a program for underprivileged children who are gifted. We also sponsor a number of scholarships in environmental studies."

He nodded as if impressed. "Then you aren't just a little rich girl."

"Is that what you thought, Kincaid?"

"Henry didn't talk about you much. Reading between the lines, though, I assumed you specialized in spending money."

"I do, but most of it on people in need."

He smiled his familiar smile. "My hat's off to you, Miss Van Dam."

She couldn't tell if he was being glib, or even if he cared what she'd said. In fact, it was hard to know what Jack Kincaid was thinking.

"I am curious about one thing," he said. "If your husband was so lazy and self-indulgent, why did you marry him?"

"I thought I loved him, of course. We came from similar backgrounds and I suppose I romanticized him. Trent Billingsly is in the past. I try not to look back, I try not to think about him anymore."

"Do you have a boyfriend?"

His directness shouldn't have surprised her, but it did. "I'm seeing someone, if that's what you mean."

"And what does he do?"

"My, you're certainly full of questions," she replied.

Jack gave a shrug. "In a small community like this, people tend to share their lives."

She smiled sweetly. "You apparently feel we should share ours."

"I admit to being curious about you," he said.

"Are you going to tell me all about your love life, too? Is that what it means to be a part of the community?"

He chuckled. "In other words, I should mind my own business."

"Take it any way you wish, Jack. I just hope you understand there are limits on how friendly I intend to get." With that, she stood and returned to the runway, walking from one end of it to the other.

3

ABOUT THE TIME SHELLEY returned to the hangar, Jack announced that he heard a vehicle approaching. He walked around the plane and Shelley followed him. The sound of a motor became distinct, then a small vehicle appeared, pushing its way through the foliage that encroached onto the double-rutted trail.

The driver was a woman, dark-headed and attractive with large almond-shaped eyes and olive skin. She looked about thirty-five. She wore a simple loose-fitting cotton sundress. Her hair was gathered into a ponytail and held by a ribbon. There was a bit of liner on her eyes and maybe a smudge of shadow. Otherwise she wore no makeup. The Jeep came to a halt beside them.

"*Voilà!*" Jack said to the new arrival. "*Ça va*, Chantal?"

The woman climbed out of the vehicle. "*Hé*, Jack. *Et toi?*" She turned to Shelley, a smile on her face, but also clearly curious about her.

Jack made the introductions and they shook hands. Chantal Favre pushed back a strand of her dark hair as she looked Shelley over. "It isn't the best circumstances for us to meet," she said in heavily accented English.

"No, it's not a happy time."

"I'm afraid, also, I have bad news, Mrs. Van Dam," she said. "Sorry to say, but somebody broke into the house of your uncle and made a terrible mess. Truly awful. We could not tell if anything was stolen."

"Who would do that?" Jack asked.

"Nobody from the island, of course," Chantal replied. "I have notified the gendarmerie on Saint Barts. They are sending somebody over here tomorrow."

Shelley looked at Jack. "Are burglaries that common here?"

"No. There's no crime on Saint Maurice at all."

"But it can't always be predicted what outsiders will do," Chantal said quickly.

"I'm not so sure this is a random thing," Jack argued.

The Frenchwoman gave him a look, which Shelley noticed but didn't understand.

"You said Uncle Henry had been worried about strangers," Shelley reminded Jack. "Do you think this is the kind of thing he was concerned about?"

"I don't know. Only Henry could answer that." After reflecting a moment, he turned to Chantal. "When did the break-in occur?"

"We don't know. Simone discovered it yesterday when she went to take vegetables from the garden since *monsieur* could no longer use them. She cleaned the house of your uncle once a week," Chantal explained to Shelley. "She is very honest, so I am sure she is not responsible. The same goes for everyone else in the village."

"I went by the house on my way to Saint Thomas," Jack said, "but that was several days ago. I didn't stop to check the place. There seemed no reason to, since it had been sealed by the police."

"Well, it has happened," Chantal said. "There is nothing we can do about it now."

"I'll load the luggage," Jack suggested. "Then we can get over there and have a look."

"Can I help?" Shelley asked.

"Oh, let him do it," Chantal interjected. "He's strong. Besides, it is very hot."

"Right," Jack intoned. "We don't want anybody sweating but me."

The women exchanged smiles.

"Have you decided what you will do with the plantation?" Chantal questioned as Jack went off. "Will you sell it, or will you live here on Saint Maurice?"

Shelley looked into the woman's dark eyes. Though Chantal was simply dressed, she had the savoir faire characteristic of Frenchwomen. There was also a familiarity between her and Jack that piqued Shelley's interest. "I won't be living here," she replied. "Beyond that, I haven't decided what to do."

Chantal glanced toward Jack, who was on the far side of the plane, gathering the luggage. She lowered her voice. "Before you make any decisions, talk first to me, Mrs. Van Dam. I don't know what Jack has told you, but his only interest is to keep things as they are here. In that sense, he is like your uncle."

"Jack hasn't spoken to me about the house."

"Not even to ask your plans?"

"No."

"That is surprising."

Jack came by with two big bags. He glanced at them. "What are you two conspiring about?"

"We are talking, not conspiring," Chantal returned. "You men are such egotists, you think you are all women wish to discuss."

He heaved the bags into the back seat of the Jeep. "I didn't say anything about me," he said.

"It was what you were thinking. Your mind is not a mystery, Jack Kincaid. So don't bother to deny it."

He gave her a look, which made Chantal laugh. Watching their easy exchange, Shelley was almost certain there was something going on between them.

By the time all her bags were in the Jeep, the entire back was filled, leaving only the two seats in front for the three of them.

"I'll walk," Jack offered. "You two go on ahead."

"*C'est fou*," Chantal said. "That's dumb. *Madame* can sit on your lap, eh?"

Jack turned to Shelley. "What do you think, *madame?*"

"Whatever works."

"*Viens*," Chantal said. "It's settled then." She climbed into the driver's seat.

Jack got in and Shelley sat on his knees, balancing herself by holding on to the top of the windshield. As they lurched forward, bouncing over the bump between the tracks, Shelley was thrown against Jack's chest. Before she could right herself, he put his arm around her middle, holding her firmly as they jolted along the rutted trail.

"Relax and enjoy the ride," he said. "It won't take long."

It was impossible to ignore his warm body. His arm felt like a band of steel around her waist. There was no question he was taking advantage of the situation. Shelley wanted to make him loosen his grip, but she knew that would only draw attention to her discomfort. Even without looking at him, she was certain that a smile was flickering at the corners of his mouth.

To distract herself, Shelley focused all her attention on the trail. Undoubtedly they must be driving along on the same path that she'd led Uncle Henry's mule over all those years ago. Rough as it was, it had been vastly improved since her last visit.

In places, thick undergrowth leaned into the road. Vines and branches hung low enough that she had to duck a few times to keep from being hit in the face. The trail wound up a slope. Sitting on the flank of the hill was the old white-stucco plantation house. It was two stories tall—imposing, though not particularly elegant. A couple of enormous shade trees grew nearby, their boughs extending over the red tile roof. In front, the small field that had once served as a kind of lawn was now overgrown with knee-high grass.

Despite the bouncing of the Jeep, Shelley could see that the house was run-down, as Jack had warned. The place was overgrown with vines, roof tiles were broken. Uncle Henry had never been fastidious, but clearly he'd let things slip.

Chantal parked in front of the house. The heavy wooden door was ajar, the lock shattered.

"You see," Chantal said. "It's terrible."

Thankful to be finally able to extricate herself, Shelley pried Jack's arm from around her waist and stepped down from the Jeep.

She stared at the crumbling facade, and tears began to well. For the first time, she experienced the reality of her uncle's death. Taking a tissue from her purse, she dabbed at her eyes.

Jack came up beside her. He put a brotherly arm around her shoulders, but didn't say a word. Chantal joined them and they stood silently for a moment, gazing at the plantation house.

"I'm very sorry for this," Chantal said, softly.

"What is, is," Shelley replied stoically. "I'll just have to deal with it."

Jack led the way up the steps, then carefully pushed the front door open. Shelley followed him into the cool, darkened entry hall. The floor was tiled, and there was a worn Oriental in the middle of it. Though it had been seventeen years, she recognized the carpet.

The slightly musty smell was familiar, instantly evoking recollections from her previous visit. Shelley glanced at the heavy wood sideboard where there had always been a huge bouquet of flowers from the garden. The cut-glass vase was still there, but it was empty now.

She stepped forward, taking a journey back in time as she inhaled. The air was dank because the thick walls kept the temperature pleasantly cool inside. There had been no need for air-conditioning. As she recalled, the sole source of electricity was a generator out back that Henry had run only intermittently.

Shelley stopped at the foot of the staircase where her uncle had fallen. She shivered at the thought of his crumpled body lying there.

As she glanced around, she realized the house could have been empty a year and it wouldn't have appeared much different. The floor was clean enough. The few pieces of furniture and the heavy wooden banister were well dusted. But the paint on the plaster walls was old and cracking. The interior of the house had been neglected as much as the outside.

Shelley went through the archway leading to the large sitting room. It was filled with the same heavy Mediterranean furniture. Except for cushions askew on the sofas and a painting lying on the floor, nothing appeared amiss.

She lingered a moment, recalling the first night she'd spent in the plantation house. After dinner she'd come to this room with her parents and Uncle Henry. They had eaten by candlelight, then Henry had cranked up the generator so that they could listen to the radio.

Her eye went to the chair in the corner where her mother had sat reading while Uncle Henry translated the news from French. The radio was still there. She stared at the place on the floor where she'd sat listening to the strange language as her uncle translated it in his booming, melodramatic voice.

"Simone told me the worst is in the library," Chantal said solemnly.

As they walked back through the house, Shelley paused at the dining room. It, too, looked as if it had been searched rather than ransacked. But the library was a disaster. Books had been pulled from the shelves and were haphazardly heaped in the middle of the room. Drawers and cabinets were open, papers scattered everywhere. Chairs were overturned, the louvered shutters were wide open, allowing in both light and the tropical air.

Jack picked his way through the mess to the window, where he secured the shutters. "This wasn't a simple burglary," he said. "I bet whoever it was, paged through every book here."

"Simone said also Monsieur Van Dam's bedroom was a mess," Chantal added. "If you want to start here, Jack, *madame* and I will go upstairs, eh?"

"Okay, fine," he replied. "I'll start cleaning up."

The women made their way back to the entry hall. Shelley paused at the foot of the stairs. "This is where they found him, wasn't it?"

"*Oui,*" the woman answered. It was barely a whisper.

Uncle Henry's life had been a mystery, even to his family. "Did you know my uncle well?" Shelley asked, hoping to find some comfort in anything she could learn about Henry.

Chantal looked sad. "Everyone knows everybody on the island. There are only thirty inhabitants here. But if you are asking if Monsieur Van Dam and I were friends, I would have to say no. He stayed very much to himself, though he was always polite. If he was close to anyone here, it was Jack."

"Because they were both Americans?"

"Perhaps. Monsieur Van Dam had a few French friends, though. He was close to a scientist from Lyon by the name of Philippe Dufour. My husband, Jean, flew the men on a joint expedition once. And Dufour has come to Saint Maurice several times to visit your uncle."

"Then your husband was the one Jack bought his plane from," Shelley said. "He mentioned someone named Jean."

"*Oui.* After Jean drowned in a diving accident, I offered the plane for sale. Jack came to look at it, and fell in love with the island. Most of the land was owned by your uncle, but Jean and I had a small cottage on the north shore that had been his grandmother's. I sold it to Jack, too. I am surprised he did not tell you this."

Something in Chantal's voice told her that Jack Kincaid may have replaced the woman's husband in more ways than one. "Our relationship is fairly limited," Shelley said. "We only met this morning."

Chantal seemed satisfied with the answer. Then she lowered her voice to make sure they weren't overheard. "I must discuss something of importance with you, Mrs. Van Dam."

"Please call me Shelley."

"And I am Chantal." She took a quick look over her shoulder before pulling an envelope from her pocket. "Some months ago your uncle gave this to me. He said I was to give it to you immediately, if he was to die. No one else was to know about it."

"Not even Jack?"

"No one."

She studied the envelope. It was limp from the humidity and wrinkled. Henry had written her name on the outside in his distinctive script. Why on earth had her uncle chosen Chantal as a courier of a posthumous message?

"Shall I read it now?"

She shrugged. "It is your business. I have done my duty in delivering it."

Shelley hesitated only a second, then tore the envelope open. The letter was written in her uncle's meticulous hand.

Shelley,

You will receive this only in the event of my death. Another copy is in the hands of my lawyer, Monsieur Voirin, but I have chosen this method to ensure that you receive my instructions at the earliest possible moment.

It is very important that my work be preserved. There is much treachery in the world, so please take care that my research does not fall into the hands of unscrupulous exploiters. There is only one knowledgeable person I trust to utilize what I have achieved, and that is Professor Philippe Dufour of the University of Lyon in France. See that he, and no one else, receives all my research materials. He can be trusted to do what is right. Your responsibility as my heir is to put it into his hands. What you do with the rest of my property, I leave to your complete discretion.

Uncle Henry

Shelley stared at the letter, her hand shaking. Then she looked up at Chantal. "Did Uncle Henry tell you what's in this letter?"

"No. Only that I should deliver it to you."

Shelley put the letter in the pocket of her pants. "I must contact Philippe Dufour immediately. How can I do that?"

"The only direct communication is by radio telephone. There is a transmitter in my home. Jack also has one."

"Is it possible to contact someone in France that way?"

"Yes."

Shelley felt a wave of doubt. If her uncle trusted Jack so much, why then hadn't he given this letter to him? On the other hand, Henry had shown a fair degree of confidence in the pilot when he gave him the journals to mail to her in the first place. Perhaps Uncle Henry had intentionally arranged his life so that no one person knew everything, leaving her with the task of fitting all the pieces together now that he was dead.

"Do you wish to see the bedroom?" Chantal asked.

"Yes, I suppose we should."

As they started up the stairs, Shelley suddenly remembered the notebooks sitting outside in the Jeep. Henry's letter had raised fresh doubt about the wisdom of bringing them to St. Maurice. Had her uncle been paranoid, or was there a real reason for concern?

At the far end of the landing there was a set of double doors leading to the master suite. They were open. Even before they got there, Shelley could see that the room was pretty well turned upside down. The contents of the armoire had been dumped onto the floor, and drawers of the dresser emptied.

"*Mon dieu,*" Chantal said. "Look at this! I will stay and help you put everything back again, if you like."

"That's very kind of you."

As they retreated along the hallway, Shelley peered into the small guest room she'd stayed in as a child. It looked about the same as it had nearly two decades earlier.

"I think I'll sleep in here," she said.

"Because of the problem, perhaps you would like to sleep at my home. This big house will be very lonely."

"No, I'd planned to stay here until I decide what to do. Thank you for inviting me, though."

"Are you sure?"

"Yes, really."

When they got back to the library, Jack had already stacked most of the books. He was standing at the library table, placing Henry's chess pieces back in a box. "Is that the set you used to play with Uncle Henry?" she asked.

He ran his fingers over the polished wood. "Yes. We'd play every Sunday evening over a bottle of port from his cellar. Usually it would be here, in this room, but occasionally at my place." He closed the lid of the box. "How were things upstairs?"

"A disaster," Chantal said. "I'm going to help Shelley with the house. Would you be a good boy and take her valises to the guest room upstairs?"

"All right." He started for the door. Then he stopped. "Oh, by the way, I checked Henry's laboratory and it's torn up, too. Many of his specimens have been removed. It's starting to look as though whoever did this was after his research." He gave Shelley a meaningful look as he left the room.

She knew he was thinking of the journals. And if Jack was right, then Henry may not have been as paranoid as they thought.

Chantal began replacing books on the shelves. Shelley joined her. As they worked, she thought about staying alone in the big old house. In spite of what she'd said, the prospect did bother her some, especially once darkness fell.

"Does the generator work?" she asked Chantal.

"I don't believe it does anymore. But we have a diesel generator on the island now. It goes on for a few hours in the morning, and at night from seven till eleven o'clock. This house is connected. After eleven, you must use the lanterns. I'm afraid we live simply here."

"You must like it, though," Shelley said. "I know Uncle Henry did."

"That was where Monsieur Van Dam and I disagreed. I talked to him many times about adding improvements, perhaps bringing in some tourism—not much, but enough to add to our incomes. I am not a rich woman, but compared to the others..."

"Obviously Uncle Henry didn't share your feelings."

"No," Chantal responded. "That's why I am very interested in your plans for the plantation."

"As I told you, I haven't made a decision yet."

Chantal glanced toward the door, her voice assuming the same conspiratorial tone as before. "If you decide to sell, I would like very much to buy the plantation from you. I will need investors, of course. I believe a resort could be built here. After you have had a chance to look around, I believe you will see the potential." She hesitated. "You will decide soon what you will do with the plantation, will you not?"

Shelley nodded.

"Don't speak of this to Jack, please," Chantal added. "He will not like my idea. It is your business, and what he thinks is not important."

Shelley was surprised. "I thought you and Jack were friends."

Chantal showed an uncharacteristic trace of embarrassment. "We are very fond of each other," she replied in a throaty tone. "But that doesn't mean we agree on all things."

They heard Jack's footsteps in the hall.

"Perhaps we can talk more of this later," she whispered. Then, speaking in a louder voice, intended for Jack's benefit, she said, "Your uncle stored many provisions, so there will be tins of food. Twice a week, when the boat came from Saint Barts, he would buy bread and fresh meat. I will bring you some tomorrow, when supplies arrive."

Jack stood in the doorway, observing them. "You don't really plan to stay here now, do you, Shelley?" he asked.

"Yes, why shouldn't I?" ·

"Something's going on, and until it's sorted out I don't think it's a good idea for you to be alone."

"I agree," Chantal said. "I offered her to stay with me, but she wouldn't accept."

Shelley laughed. "You're both very kind. I'm sure I'll be fine." She said it without conviction. Nevertheless everything was so confusing that she didn't want to rely on anyone but herself. Nor did she want to be in anyone's debt.

Jack studied her for a moment, then said, "Your bags are upstairs. Before I go, I'll straighten up the laboratory. It's in bad shape. Someone went through the pots, dumping them in the middle of the floor."

"I appreciate your help," Shelley said. "Both of you."

After he'd gone Chantal said, "I think he is truly concerned for you."

"I wouldn't be too sure about that. He's already told me I remind him of his ex-wife."

Her eyes widened. "He told you about Beth?"

"In passing," Shelley replied, giving Chantal a quick look to see how she would react. Clearly, with only a handful of people on the island, how could an attractive single man and an attractive single woman not get involved eventually?

Chantal let a long silent moment pass. Then they went to work again. In twenty minutes, all the books were back on the shelf. Chantal wiped her brow and dropped down to rest for a moment in a threadbare armchair. "Whoever did this should be taken before the firing squad and shot," she said.

"Do you have any idea at all who might have done it?"

"*Pas du tout.* None at all. Your uncle's affairs, I knew nothing about."

"Whatever they were after, I don't think they found it," Shelley observed.

"Why do you say that?"

"Just a hunch."

Chantal seemed to think about that for a minute. Then she said, "*Tiens*, should we fix some lunch? We can probably find something in the pantry. A tin of pâté, some crackers. And Monsieur Van Dam's wine cellar was a very good one. If you don't mind, of course."

"Well," Jack said, as he entered the library, "you two sitting down on the job?"

"*Voilà!*" Chantal exclaimed. "Just in time. We are considering making some lunch. What do you think?"

"Not for me. I've got to run. But I got the worst of the mess cleaned up in the lab. If you come across some heavy work that needs doing, I can take care of it tomorrow."

Shelley contemplated him, fascinated by his rough charm, his sometimes-friendly, sometimes-combative demeanor. "You've been very helpful, Jack," she said. "I appreciate it."

He shrugged off her thanks. "We're neighbors, at least for a while. And on Saint Maurice that means something, eh, Chantal?"

Chantal, who was hugging her knees to her chest, smiled faintly. "Of course."

Shelley's gaze fell on the chess set. "Oh, by the way," she said, "since you were Uncle Henry's chess partner, why don't you take the set? I'm sure he'd want you to have it."

"That's very kind, but don't you want it?"

"I have my father's. I don't need another one." She picked up the box and the heavy inlaid board and handed them to him. "I'll see you to the door."

"*Ciao*, Chantal," he called over his shoulder as they walked away.

"*À bientôt*," she replied.

Shelley went with Jack to the entry hall, neither of them speaking. Then she said, "Chantal's very nice, isn't she?"

"She can be charming as hell."

"Are you having an affair with her?" Shelley asked abruptly. It had come out of her mouth before she'd had time to censor the thought, and now she was embarrassed. "Please forget I asked you that."

He was grinning with such amusement that Shelley had to look away.

"We aren't having an affair," he said evenly.

"It really doesn't matter if you are or not. I just—"

"Well, we aren't, though I admit our friendship has evolved over the years."

"You don't need to explain."

"Then why did you ask?"

Exasperated, she headed for the door and went out onto the veranda. She was more angry with herself than she was with him. She hoped that by walking away, she could induce him to let the matter drop. Jack sauntered out the door and stood beside her. She ignored him and stared out at the band of blue sea over the tops of the trees.

Shelley had forgotten about the view. It was more pleasant than spectacular. The plantation house had been built far enough up the slope to afford a perspective of the sea, though the trees at the foot of the field and the advancing jungle blocked some of the view. Her uncle had told her that at one time there had been cane fields all around, but those had long since become fallow. Now, even the house seemed to be succumbing to the onslaught of nature.

"Why did Henry let this place get so run-down?" she asked.

"I suppose it wasn't important to him to keep it up."

"It was in much better shape when I was here before."

"The house wasn't as old, then, and neither was Henry. Frankly, I don't think anything much mattered to the old boy except his work and his plants. The purpose of the roof was to keep his head dry."

"What do you think I should do with the plantation?" she asked.

"That's your decision."

"I know that. If you were to advise me, what would you recommend?"

"Personally, I'd like things to stay just as they are. But you're not me, and what I think doesn't matter."

She gave him a sideward glance. Had he guessed what Chantal had said to her? Or was he just being honest? "Perhaps whoever buys it will decide," she commented, testing him.

Jack said nothing. He was staring out at the aqua sea.

"Beautiful, isn't it?" she remarked after several moments.

"A nice day for sailing."

"Do you like to sail?"

"I have a boat. It's anchored in the cove by my house."

"Chantal told me she'd sold you the house that belonged to her husband's grandmother."

"Yes, it's the perfect place for a crotchety old bachelor."

"Are you crotchety?"

He laughed. "You'll have to come see my place sometime."

Shelley didn't respond. Jack turned to her and said, "Well, I'd better be going. Thanks for the chess set. I'll treasure it."

"Thanks for the ride this morning, and for your help cleaning up." She stuck out her hand.

Jack took it, holding her hand an extra-long time. "I don't suppose you'll change your mind about staying here."

"I'm a big girl, Jack. There's no need to worry."

He reached out and touched her cheek in an affectionate way. She liked the contrast of the roughness of his skin against the smoothness of hers. "You're the boss." Then he went down the steps, stopped and said, "Whoever broke in doesn't know you have the notebooks with you, so you're probably safe. But if something does happen, or you get scared, feel free to come to my place. It's on the water, half a mile down the road," he said, pointing. "All you have to do is follow the track. It ends at my door."

Shelley didn't know how to take his comments. Was his remark about the danger calculated to send her running to his protective embrace, or was he genuinely concerned? "I'm sure that won't be necessary," she said. "Thanks anyway."

He nodded. She watched him head down the road. Jack Kincaid was a loner and an adventurer, a man bent on the singular life he'd staked out for himself, no matter the consequences. Admittedly, despite her determined resistance, she was intrigued.

"Jack's a charmer."

She turned at the sound of Chantal's voice. Chantal was leaning against the doorjamb, a knowing smile on her lips. Shelley sensed hostility in her demeanor, as though Jack were a bone of contention between them. Or was she only imagining it? "He's different, I'll grant him that."

"You can't let him deceive you, Shelley."

"What do you mean, 'deceive'?"

"Don't think he is as indifferent as he acts. Jack is a survivor," Chantal said, "the same as me. He knows what he wants, and he usually figures out how to get it."

"I'm no fool, Chantal."

"No, I hope very much that you aren't."

They exchanged looks, a kind of mutual sizing up. There was something in Chantal that seemed on edge for the first time since they'd met. Jack was not just a side issue. And yet Chantal didn't seem eager for a confrontation. To the contrary, her expression softened, her smile turned friendly.

"You know," she said, "there is no need for us to eat lunch here. If you wish to telephone to Monsieur Dufour, let's go to my house now and we can eat there. I can also give you some provisions."

"That's very generous. But I want to be back before dark so that I can unpack and get set up."

"Of course, if this is what you want. Why are you so stubborn about staying in this house?"

"Let's just say I feel duty-bound to protect what my uncle accomplished here."

Chantal was obviously perplexed by the comment, but she didn't ask for clarification. "Whatever you wish."

Shelley followed her into the house, very much aware of her sensuality. Chantal had a natural allure, and it was not at all surprising that she and Jack had been lovers. It would have been surprising if they hadn't been.

"Let's get our things and go, okay?" Chantal said.

"Fine."

"Do you need anything besides your purse?"

"No."

Shelley would have liked to bring along the suitcase with the notebooks, but they were too heavy to lug around. And, as Jack had said, nobody but the two of them knew the journals were back on the island. They should be safe in her room—assuming, of course, that Jack Kincaid could be trusted.

4

BY THE TIME THEY PILED into the Jeep, whatever tension there had been between them had dissipated. Chantal was laughing and in a lighthearted mood. She kept up a constant stream of chatter as she drove, her ponytail flying in the breeze.

When they went past the airstrip neither of them said a word about Jack, though Shelley couldn't help thinking of the way he had held on to her so possessively on their ride to the plantation house. That was the aspect of Jack she didn't trust, but couldn't get out of her mind.

"If we make Henry's house a *pension*," the Chantal said, "we need to improve the road. It would be less than two kilometers altogether. It wouldn't be so expensive."

It was pretty clear that Chantal intended to pursue her plan for the property. She was already sounding assumptive. Shelley didn't know why, but she found herself resisting the idea, perhaps out of protective feelings for her uncle, his home and the life he'd made on Saint Maurice. Deep down, though, she suspected Jack also had something to do with it.

Why his desires should matter to her, Shelley didn't know. He offered no solution to her problem, whereas Chantal did. Which only went to show how out of touch Jack was, even compared to his neighbors on the island. Why shouldn't a modest little resort of some kind be built? He could profit from the tourist dollars as much as anyone.

They broke out of the forest and came upon the bay. The road ran along the beach, a lovely stretch of sand that was completely deserted. The first of the dozen-or-so scattered homes lay just ahead. It was a tiny house with a corrugated-steel roof festooned with flowering vines. The yard was filled with decorative pottery. An old woman sitting on a straight-backed chair by the door gawked as they passed. Chantal tooted the horn and waved.

"You must meet everyone," she said. "But not today. Better if I organize something. Everyone will want to meet Monsieur Van Dam's niece."

"Whatever you think," Shelley replied.

The next house was Chantal's. It was much larger than the one they'd passed and was surrounded by a low wall that enclosed the garden. There was no gate, so they pulled directly into the enclosure, stopping abruptly at the end of the drive.

The structure was white stucco with a tile roof. The windows on either side of the door had bright green shutters. Pink bougainvillea covered half of the front of the house and there were flowers in terra-cotta pots all along the porch that ran the full width of the house.

"What a lovely house!" Shelley exclaimed as they got out of the Jeep.

"Jean built it after we were married. We lived in it four years together before he was killed."

"How sad."

"I am surprised I am here this long," Chantal said. "I thought I would return to France, but then things happened and I stayed."

Shelley knew without elaboration what "things" had happened.

They went to the front door, which was unlocked. Chantal said, "Welcome," as she gestured for her to enter.

The interior was clean and simple. The wood furniture in the living area was mostly modern and functional, though there were one or two antique pieces. Chantal had a good sense of color, which showed in her many oil paintings. There was a vase of flowers on the sideboard, and a large pottery bowl on the dining table at the far end of the room, overflowing with fruit. Twin ceiling fans turned slowly overhead.

"A very cheerful room," Shelley commented.

"I live alone," Chantal said, "but I try not to act like it." She walked toward what looked like the door to the kitchen. "What will you drink? I have wine, beer, mineral water."

"Mineral water would be fine."

"I have no ice just now. I hope you don't mind."

"So long as it's wet, it doesn't matter."

"Make yourself at home," Chantal said, disappearing into the kitchen.

Shelley sat on the sofa, which afforded a view of the bay. From the window, she could see where their boat had anchored on her first trip to Saint Maurice. Staring placidly at the scene, she passed a nostalgic moment remembering her parents.

Chantal returned with a glass of mineral water for each of them and sat down next to her. *"Santé,"* she said, touching Shelley's glass.

They each took a sip.

"Perhaps I should try to reach Monsieur Dufour before it is too late to call," Chantal suggested. "We can eat after, then we will return to the plantation house and I will help you straighten the rest of the mess."

"You're devoting an awful lot of time to me," Shelley said. "I hate to impose."

"You are my neighbor. Soon I hope I can say you are my friend." They each smiled and Chantal said, "I will try now to telephone."

Chantal went to a desk in the corner of the room. Shelley leaned back, trying to decide how to approach Philippe Dufour. The best solution, it seemed, was to be direct. Uncle Henry had wanted her to turn his life's work over to the man, and presumably the Frenchman would know what to do with it.

When Chantal finally made the connection, she called Shelley to the desk and handed her the phone.

"Professor Dufour," she began, "I am Henry Van Dam's niece, Shelley, and I'm calling you from Saint Maurice."

"Yes, *madame*, Henry spoke of you," the man replied warily. "What a great surprise, indeed."

"Professor, are you aware that my uncle passed away recently?"

"Henry is dead? *Mon Dieu!* Was it his heart?"

"No. An accident. He fell down the stairs."

"I am so sorry to hear this, *madame*. It is a most grievous shock for me, and certainly for you, too."

"Naturally I was very upset. I'm calling because my uncle has given me the responsibility of settling his affairs. I must dispose of his professional papers and his research."

"Yes . . ."

"And Uncle Henry wanted you to have everything—his life's work, in effect."

"*Vraiment?* You are serious?"

"Yes, Professor. Didn't my uncle give you any indication?"

"Henry and I were very close for many years, *madame*, but I had no idea. I mean—"

"The problem, Professor Dufour, is that I haven't had the opportunity yet to investigate everything, and I have no idea what is valuable and what isn't. Would you be willing to assist me in evaluating his papers and things?"

"I will certainly do what I can, Miss Van Dam."

"Within a day or two I will be meeting with Uncle Henry's lawyer, Mr. Voirin," she continued. "If he approves, I would like to dispose of the research materials immediately. My uncle was most eager for you to have them. In fact, he regarded it as urgent."

"I see."

Shelley glanced at Chantal, who, though across the room, was clearly within hearing range. Shelley decided to choose her words carefully. "Professor, may I ask you a question?"

"Certainly, *madame*."

"Uncle Henry was convinced that someone was determined to exploit his work in some way. I have no idea what or who he was afraid of, and I would have dismissed it as a product of his . . . eccentricity . . . except that sometime before my arrival his house here on Saint Maurice was burglarized. We think his work was the object of the crime."

"A burglary?"

"Yes. We think some of his laboratory specimens may have been taken. Can you explain who might have been behind this and what they wanted?"

"No, Miss Van Dam, I have no idea. Henry was very secretive about his work, as you may know. I cannot say with certainty what the object of his most recent researches were."

"Well, perhaps we'll discover the answer in his papers. Would you be willing to come to Saint Maurice?"

"If I can be of assistance, certainly. I could be there in a few days, if I am able to make travel arrangements."

"That would be excellent. I can't tell you how glad I will be to put his notebooks in safe hands."

"Notebooks, *madame?*"

Shelley hadn't intended to let that out just yet. "His papers, I mean. At the moment, much of it is in a heap on the floor. There's also the possibility that other things will turn up."

"Such as?"

"It seems likely some of his more valuable work was put away for safekeeping." Shelley could see Chantal listening to her every word.

"Quite right," Philippe Dufour said.

"But I'm sure it will all turn up."

"Henry was most passionate about his work. I'm sure he'd be concerned that nothing was lost."

"I agree," Shelley replied, watching Chantal sip her water. "Can I help with arrangements for you here, Professor?"

"No, I have traveled to that part of the world many times. But if you would be so kind, please give me a number where I can reach you, Miss Van Dam."

"I'll put my friend, Mrs. Favre, on the line so she can tell you. I'm calling from her house."

Chantal picked up the phone and spoke with Philippe Dufour. When she'd conveyed the necessary information, she hung up.

"Thank you, Chantal," Shelley said. "I feel much better."

"Then all is well?"

"I'm sure it will be in a few days."

"*Bien.* Shall we have lunch, then? Perhaps a glass of wine to celebrate. What do you think?"

"To be honest," Shelley responded, "I think that sounds like an excellent idea."

IT WAS MIDAFTERNOON before they'd made it back to the plantation house. The first thing Shelley did was make sure that the suitcase containing the notebooks was still there. To her great relief everything was as she had left it.

Then she and Chantal went to work, putting the house in order. They straightened everything except the master bedroom. Shelley decided to leave that for later, since she would have to go through her uncle's personal effects, anyway. The only thing they did in there was take down the mosquito netting and move it to the small guest room.

By five o'clock they were sitting down on the overstuffed chairs in the salon. "It is a job, this house," Chantal observed.

"Maybe Uncle Henry is to be forgiven. It would be expensive to keep this place in good repair, and he was not a rich man."

"I often wondered where his money came from."

"My grandparents were quite wealthy. I think Henry lived off his inheritance. I don't know if he ever earned any money of consequence."

"Was he due to inherit more soon?"

"No. He got everything years ago, as my father did."

"That's strange," Chantal remarked, furrowing her brow. "When I discussed improvements to the road and the electrical system with him last year, he said he couldn't afford to pay. But he said that in another year it would be possible because he was expecting a large sum of money."

Shelley was perplexed by the comment. "I have no idea what he could have been referring to."

"Perhaps he had some business you are not aware of," Chantal suggested.

"Maybe."

"You know," Chantal said, looking as though she'd just remembered something, "I asked this when Henry had a visitor. In fact, I recall now that the guest was Monsieur Dufour."

"The professor?"

"Yes. The same. And I remember something else. It was Jack who flew Monsieur Dufour here the last time he came."

An odd feeling went through Shelley. Jack had never mentioned Philippe Dufour. Of course, there may not be any reason why he should, especially since he wasn't aware of the letter Chantal had given her.

"Well," Chantal said, rising. "I have things to attend to. Perhaps we can take an inventory in the kitchen now, so I will know what you need. Then I must go."

They went through the pantry and made a list of the supplies Shelley would need from the next boat. Then Chantal showed her how to operate the butane stove and the electric water pump.

"When the electricity comes on tonight, be sure to pump water, if you want a shower before you go to bed. Otherwise you will have to wait till morning."

They discussed other practical matters. When Shelley said she'd like to have the house dusted and swept out, Chantal agreed to arrange for Simone Roche, the woman who'd cleaned weekly for Uncle Henry, to come by the next day.

Having done all they could, they went out onto the veranda. A sea breeze was blowing strongly. Chantal pushed back a strand of her dark hair.

"There's a wind, but it's still warm," she remarked.

"Yes," Shelley replied. "I'm dying to get in the shower."

"Maybe there is water in the cistern from before. You can try." She held out her hand. "I must go. It is good to have you on Saint Maurice, but I am sorry you came under such sad circumstances."

"You've been very kind, Chantal. Thank you for everything."

"Think about my idea for the house."

"Yes, I will."

Chantal smiled and got in the Jeep. After she started the engine, she said, "If you are afraid to be here alone, go to Jack. I'm sure he will be glad to see you." Then she waved, and drove off in the late-afternoon sun.

The comment caught Shelley completely off guard. Why was Chantal suddenly promoting Jack? And what did she mean, he would be glad to see her? Had she seen something Shelley hadn't? Or was it simply that she knew the man better?

Long after the Jeep had disappeared down the road, Shelley remained on the veranda, fighting the uneasy feeling that had gripped her. Chantal Favre was a confounding individual. She could be kind and inspire trust one moment, then cast doubt on everything the next. The real issue was, Shelley didn't trust her motives. Maybe Chantal wanted Uncle Henry's house too badly—enough to sacrifice other things that mattered to her, even Jack Kincaid.

Shelley turned and faced the shattered front door. With Uncle Henry dead, the house was hers now, but she wished it wasn't. She wished she was at home in Los Angeles. She wished she hadn't come to Saint Maurice.

Such thoughts were hardly productive. She *was* there, and she had a job to do. Bracing herself emotionally, she went back inside.

The old house seemed even darker and more forbidding now that she was alone. The dankness in the entry hall made her shiver. Shelley couldn't bring herself to look at the staircase where Henry had fallen, so she went into the sitting room where she had passed many happy hours with her parents and uncle.

The late-afternoon sun cast deep shadows in the room. Though Shelley knew the electricity wasn't scheduled to come on yet, she went to the old console radio she'd listened to as a girl and turned it on. After the click, there was nothing. The radio was as dead as her uncle. She'd known it would be, but something had made her try anyway.

She sat down in her mother's chair, watching particles of dust floating in the angled rays of the sun. It was so terribly quiet. Shelley regretted she hadn't had the foresight to bring a transistor radio—anything to liven her spirits.

After several more minutes of wallowing in melancholy, Shelley decided to take charge of herself. She hadn't done much more than glance in the laboratory while she and Chantal were straightening everything, so she would take a look at it now, while there was still enough light to see.

The lab was really a sort of conservatory-solarium at the back of the house. It was where Henry had grown his plants and conducted his experiments. Jack had swept out the place, having dumped most of the debris that had been on the floor in a pile outside the back door. The remaining plants looked forlorn, making her suspect that the burglars might have removed many specimens. Whoever had broken in was obviously intent on finding something. What could Uncle Henry have been working on to create such interest?

Shelley left the laboratory. What she really wanted right now was to take a nice long shower. It wasn't important that the water be hot, so long as there was enough for a good scrubbing and a shampoo.

The gigantic bathroom upstairs had been added years after the original structure was built, though it was at least seventy-five years old. The fixtures seemed ancient. A small electric water heater mounted on the white tile wall provided the only hot water in the house. Without electricity, though, it was useless.

Shelley turned on the tap, delighted to discover there was water. Thrilled, she got toiletries and some underwear from her room, then returned to the bath and quickly stripped. The shower was a bit primitive, but it felt like heaven. The stream began to wane as she was rinsing off, then it stopped abruptly. But she'd lucked out—the water hadn't run out while she was all lathered up.

Shelley dried herself and brushed the tangles from her hair, realizing she would have to let it dry naturally. Back in her room she put on a white satin nightgown. She would go downstairs and fix herself a light meal of canned fruit, and the pâté and crackers Chantal had brought back with them. Then, once the electricity came on, she would try Uncle Henry's big console radio again.

She made her way down the stairs, which were quite dark, considering the time of day. There was still some sunlight outside, but it was fading rapidly. The kitchen was better lit than the hallway, so she knew she'd have no trouble preparing her dinner. She'd laid everything out on the counter and had just turned for the cupboard when a flicker of motion at the window caught her eye. A man had walked past.

Shelley had only the briefest glimpse of him. He had a swarthy complexion, with a stubble of beard on his jaw and a hat pulled down low over his eyes. He was gone in an instant, having passed by without so much as looking in. For a moment, Shelley couldn't breathe. She instantly thought of the burglars.

Her next thought was that she had no gun, nothing she could use to defend herself. The house couldn't even be locked. If the man was bent on entering, it would be no problem for him to do so. Though there were countless dangers in Los Angeles, she would have felt so much safer there, knowing she could at least pick up a telephone and call for help.

Pulling herself together, Shelley rummaged through the drawers until she found a butcher knife. Her heart pounding, she crept into the hall and made her way toward the back of the house, in the direction the man had taken. If he came in, she would confront him and scare him off, if she could.

She wished now she hadn't put on her nightgown. If not a burglar, the intruder could be a rapist or a murderer. Anything was possible. When she got to the conservatory, she spotted the man again. He wasn't large—actually a bit on the short side—but was definitely unsavory. He wore a tattered old suit-coat and an open-necked shirt.

He was poking through the mound of plants and mulch that Jack had left outside when he cleaned the laboratory. Since the room was almost entirely glass, it was easy to observe the stranger's actions. The door closing off the conservatory from the rest of the house was also glass, but with it so dark inside, she knew she wouldn't be seen easily.

The man outside was single-mindedly picking through the pile, looking for something.

He was perhaps in his forties, rather oafish and coarse-looking. He used his hands like a laborer, shucking aside pot fragments and plants. Finally, he stood and turned toward the conservatory. Shelley shrank into the shadows but kept her eye on him. As he moved toward the door, her fist tightened on the handle of the knife.

He pressed his face against the outside glass and peered in. He was evidently having difficulty seeing in because he had to shield his eyes from the outside light.

Shelley saw his hand move toward the doorknob, testing it. To her utter dismay, the door swung open. For a few moments the stranger just stood there. She could see his face quite plainly. The poor man was cursed with unattractive features, including what looked to be a harelip.

When he started through the open door Shelley moved out of sight, flattening her back against the wall. She stared down at the door handle, waiting for it to move, waiting for him to enter the house. She was shaking with fear, imagining all sorts of horrors.

So far as she could tell, he wasn't carrying a weapon. At least, he wasn't brandishing one. She would have an advantage in that respect. But what if he wasn't alone? What if a friend was coming in the other side of the house?

She was still waiting for the inner door to open, but it didn't. Instead, she heard movement in the laboratory. Shelley risked a glimpse through the glass door.

He was at a worktable in the center of the room, intensely searching through a number of potted plants. He lifted one from the center of the table, a strange grin on his face. Then he glanced toward the inner door. Shelley was almost positive he had seen her.

But the man abruptly turned and lumbered out into the dusk, leaving the door open behind him. He disappeared around the corner of the house.

Fearing he might be going to the front door, Shelley raced back toward it. She arrived breathless in the entry hall and hid behind the broken front door, the butcher knife clenched in her fist, raised and ready to strike. But he didn't come.

After waiting ten minutes, her ears attuned to every sound, Shelley finally let the knife drop to her side. She knew she wouldn't be able to sleep a wink knowing the guy could return and enter the place at will. There was only one solution—she had to get out of there.

She raced upstairs, pulled off her nightgown and slipped into a pair of shorts and a shirt. Dusk was rapidly approaching, but if she hurried she could make it to Jack Kincaid's place before dark.

She would take Uncle Henry's journals with her. The suitcase was heavy, but she couldn't risk leaving them behind. Grabbing the bag in one hand and the knife in the other, Shelley made her way down the stairs. She opened the front door, half expecting the intruder to be waiting on the veranda. She stepped outside, scanning the edge of the jungle.

The sun had set and the sky out over the water was magnificent. Still, it was not the time to enjoy the view. She had to get to Jack's before dark—hopefully in one piece, and with the journals in hand.

Shelley took off down the double-rutted trail. The case was heavy, very heavy, which prevented her from running. She moved as fast as she could, looking back over her shoulder, afraid that the intruder would be in hot pursuit. He wasn't.

After a couple of hundred yards at a trot, Shelley stopped for a minute to rest and shift the case to her other hand. She kept her eyes on the trail. All was quiet. In fact, the jungle seemed benign.

A tropical forest at twilight, she realized, was a wonder to behold. The lacy canopy of branches overhead let in just enough light to see, but at the same time closed out the world. As she rested, she listened to the chirping of the frogs. She recalled that on her first visit to Saint Maurice she had assumed that the noise came from thousands of birds in the jungle. Her uncle had explained that the soprano chirp was not from a bird at all, but rather from a species of frog common in the Caribbean.

Shelley's breathing had evened out, so she picked up the case again and strode off, this time at a more moderate pace. Even though it was rapidly growing darker, the trail was easy enough to follow. Because of the ruts, it could probably be negotiated in total darkness.

Half a mile wasn't all that far, but between the weight of the case and her fear that the stranger would pounce on her at any moment, Shelley felt like she'd gone the length of the Oregon Trail. Finally, though, the jungle began to thin and she came out into the open. The sea was just ahead. A cliff ran along the shore some thirty or forty feet above the breakers.

A small house sat on the point. She was able to see its roofline silhouetted clearly against the sky. There were no lights on, though it was now past seven and the island's electrical generator was in operation.

Shelley continued along the trail, feeling some relief at last, though the thought crossed her mind that Jack Kincaid might not be home. However, the prospect of having to wait for him was not nearly so frightening as being alone up at the big house, knowing an intruder was lurking in the nearby jungle.

The case had gotten so heavy that she was stopping every twenty yards or so. When she arrived at the house there was no sign of life, though the front door was open. The place was hardly more than a cottage. A picket fence enclosed the tiny flower garden. Shelley could smell the blossoms as she set the case down at the doorstep.

"Hello, Jack?" she called. "Anybody home?" Shelley waited, but there was no answer. "Jack?"

Nothing. Total silence. He wasn't home.

Glancing back up the road, Shelley saw nothing—not the intruder, no one. She couldn't decide whether to enter Jack's house or not. But the front door was wide open, practically inviting her to come in.

Her curiosity drew her inside. There was enough light to see the cottage was neat and homey, which surprised her. Somehow she'd pictured it to look more like a barracks, a place where Jack camped, rather than lived. The furniture was simple but the ambience warm. There was a large bookcase against one wall, crammed with books. That surprised her, too. Jack Kincaid did not strike her as the type who read. He seemed more like a libertine, a man wed to his pleasures. She'd pictured him spending his evenings in bed with a bottle of rum and a woman, if one was available.

More curious than ever, she looked around. To one side of the main room there was a kitchen, to the other a door that she assumed led to the bedroom. Out back, a large covered terrace with a table and chairs overlooked the sea. Clutching the butcher knife, Shelley walked out for a look.

"Jack?" she said again, thinking he might be there. But there was no response.

She stood at the edge of the terrace. Several miles out, the lights of a passing ship shone in the falling night. Even farther away she could see the mountainous profile of Saint Martin on the horizon. It was truly a breathtaking sight. Nothing in Malibu even came close.

A path led toward the edge of the precipice. She walked along it until she saw that it led down to a cove that was tucked on the opposite side of the point. A good-size sailboat was anchored in the harbor. There was a light on the craft. Was Jack aboard?

Just then her eye caught a flicker of motion in the water below. She realized someone was swimming. The cove was almost like a private pool, and she was sure the swimmer was Jack Kincaid.

Shelley felt much better, knowing Jack was nearby. She considered calling out to him, but since there was no immediate danger she decided against disturbing him. She'd wait until he returned to the house. In the meantime, she elected to watch.

At first she could only see the motion of his limbs in the translucent water. Jack was swimming the breaststroke at a leisurely pace. When he reached his boat, he clambered up a ladder hanging over the side and onto the deck. She could only see the vaguest outline of his physique, but the sight—or the suggestion of nudity—took her breath away.

She knew she was wrong to spy. If their situations were reversed, she would have been incensed. And yet she couldn't pull away. Her cheeks flushed as she stared at his body. Finally, when he stepped into the cabin, she retreated up the path.

She returned to the house and sat down on one of the chairs under the covered patio, waiting for Jack to return.

Seeing him naked had changed things. How could she look at him now and keep that sensual image of him in the water from popping into her head?

About ten minutes later, she saw a figure coming up the path. It was Jack, and he appeared to be clothed. He was whistling in a carefree sort of way. Suddenly he stopped.

"Is that you Chantal?" he called out.

Shelley's stomach clenched. Somehow, his assuming that she was Chantal made the situation worse. Despite her experience with the intruder, she wanted to run back to the plantation house as fast as she could. But she didn't have that option.

Instead she slowly rose from her chair and said, "No, Jack. It's me, Shelley."

5

As he approached, Shelley could see that his chest was bare, though he was wearing trunks. Jack stopped at the edge of the patio and peered into the shadows.

"Shelley, what are you doing here? Is something wrong?"

"Yes," she said.

Jack walked right up to her, concern registered on his face. "What's happened?"

Her heart started pounding even harder. He was so close that she could see the droplets of water on his skin. And when she inhaled, she noticed that he smelled of the sea. "I'm sorry to barge in on you like this," she began uncertainly, "but there was an intruder hanging around the plantation house and I didn't feel very safe alone. I was concerned about Uncle Henry's notebooks, too, so I brought them along for safekeeping."

"Wait a minute. You say you had an intruder?"

"Yes, a man. He entered Uncle Henry's laboratory and took a plant." She proceeded to describe in detail what had happened.

"What did this guy look like?" he asked, resting his hand on her shoulder.

Shelley found his touch unnerving, though it was undoubtedly meant to reassure her. She fidgeted, looking up at him, barely able to see the contours of his features. Her heart was still pounding—as badly as when she'd spotted the intruder, but the cause was entirely different.

Shelley took a deep breath, knowing she had to pull herself together. She gave Jack an exact description of the man and when she was finished she saw him smile, his teeth gleaming in the dark.

"I hate to say this, honey, but I think the man you saw was Claude Perrin."

"Who's that?"

"One of the villagers. He's a deaf-mute. Claude's harmless, though I admit he looks a bit sinister, poor guy."

"Well, what was he doing lurking around Uncle Henry's? And why did he come in like that and take a plant?"

"Henry raised a few orchids in addition to his experimental stuff. Claude saw one once and went wild over it, so your uncle gave him a plant of his own that Claude kept in the conservatory, with the others. Claude would go there once a week to water and fertilize it and so forth."

"Oh, my God," Shelley said, seeing that she'd misinterpreted a harmless episode. "It never occurred to me that the guy could be innocent. I thought Uncle Henry didn't associate with anyone on the island besides you."

"He didn't, much. Claude was the exception. Henry took him in like he was a stray. Actually the poor guy virtually is one. He lived with his mother until she died last year. She was the only one who could communicate with him. The villagers tolerate Claude, though none of them have much to do with him. Nobody but his mother could sign. I tried to befriend him, but he was never very receptive. I think he sensed Henry's own eccentricity and was drawn to it."

"You're suggesting that when Claude heard about the burglary he got concerned about his plant and went to see if it was all right."

"I doubt anyone was able to communicate to Claude everything that's happened, but of course he knew Henry was dead. Got very agitated about it, as a matter of fact."

"I feel like such a fool," she muttered.

Jack took her by the shoulders, smiling benevolently. Then he gathered her to his chest and gave her a big hug. Shelley was caught off guard. She had been struggling to come to terms with the effect he was having on her, and now she found herself in his arms.

"You had no way of knowing," Jack said, rubbing her back. "Claude can be pretty frightening for anybody who doesn't know him. I'm sure I would have reacted the same way under the circumstances."

Shelley was fairly sure that Jack had no idea what he was doing to her. His lean, muscular body smelled of nature and the outdoors. She savored it for a moment before gently extricating herself from his arms.

"Understandable or not," she replied, "I feel pretty dumb. I lugged those journals all the way down here for nothing."

"Maybe it's a good thing you did. You can leave them here for safekeeping."

Was Jack as innocent as he sounded, or did he want the journals in his possession for some unknown reason? He did claim to have been the one who mailed them to her. Perhaps that wasn't true.

"No," she said, moving back a step. "I think I'll take them back with me. They're my responsibility."

"Well, it's true that you and I are the only ones who know they're here. Still, that break-in concerns me. Somebody must be pretty desperate."

Shelley thought of the letter that Chantal had given her and her telephone conversation with Philippe Dufour. Before long, she would be turning the notebooks over to the Frenchman and her worries would be over. Should she tell Jack that or not? For the moment, she decided not to.

"Whoever committed that burglary is probably long gone," she said, moving even farther away from him. "I've got the journals and whatever secret they contain, so things are just as they were before Claude showed up and I panicked."

"No, they aren't the same. Now you're here with me instead of up at the plantation house alone."

Shelley could just imagine Jack's smug expression. He was probably feeling as if everything had worked out perfectly, exactly as he had planned. But what he apparently didn't realize was that her being here and her succumbing to him were not quite the same thing. Just because she'd been a little carried away by his physical appeal, didn't mean she'd let herself fall into his trap.

She assumed an innocent demeanor. "The light's almost gone. I'd better get going."

"Nonsense. There's no point in going back."

"I certainly can't stay here."

"Why not? The sofa makes into a daybed. Anyway, you know how I feel about you staying in that house alone."

She laughed, feeling the self-satisfaction of someone who was a step ahead of their adversary. She knew damned well what he was thinking.

"There's no point in trying to frighten me, Jack. When there's a reason, I do a pretty good job of it myself. Otherwise I wouldn't be here."

"I'm certainly not going to twist your arm," he said. "There's no point in running off, though. Since you're here, you might as well stay for dinner."

That was pretty transparent, too. A dinner by candlelight, some wine, a walk in the sea air, some friendly affection that soon became more than that. Who was he trying to kid?

"Who are you trying to kid?" Shelley heard the words come out of her mouth and was as surprised by them as he must have been.

"Pardon?"

Well, she'd said it. And she felt it, too, so she might as well stop playing games and say exactly what she was thinking. "You said 'stay for dinner.' Isn't what you really mean stay for sex? That's the real purpose of the invitation, isn't it?"

"What a minute," he said scratching his forehead. "Did I miss something?"

"Come on, Jack, we're both adults. You want to go to bed with me. Why not be up-front about it?"

"Well . . . I have been known to succumb to the charms of an attractive woman, but—"

"Don't pussyfoot around. You've been thinking about it since we got to Saint Maurice. Maybe before."

"I'm afraid I'm a bit confused," he said. "Are you propositioning me, or are you accusing me of propositioning you?"

"Jack!"

He chuckled. "I take that to indicate the latter."

"Can't you see I'm trying to let you know I'm not interested in that kind of relationship? I'm trying to show you the respect of being honest and straightforward."

"I thought I'd invited you to dinner, but if you wish to refuse an invitation to go to bed, that's fine by me. So what about dinner?"

She stood there, reappraising what had just happened. Maybe she *had* misread the situation—or at the very least overreacted. "We're really talking about dinner?"

"Yes," he replied. "Unless food and sex are so inextricably related in your mind that I can't mention one without implying the other."

Shelley colored, glad it was too dark to be seen. "This conversation is getting out of control."

"You brought it up."

"I was just trying to be aboveboard."

"I think I understand your moral code," he said. "What I'm less clear on is your appetite . . . for food. Do you care to have dinner with me or don't you?"

She studied him in the dark, thinking she'd made her point even if she'd been clumsy. Of course, who was to say if it had done any good? "As long as you understand where I'm coming from, I'll be happy to stay for dinner. How's that?"

"If you can trust yourself, my dear, you can certainly trust me."

She laughed. "Tell me honestly, Jack, how many times have you used that line?"

"I believe it's a first."

"I hope your cooking is more credible than you are," she told him.

"Shall we go inside and find out?" He took her hand and led her toward the dark interior. "You haven't seen my house, have you?"

"I walked through it when I arrived."

"Well, let's get a lamp lit so you can see. Wait here." Jack let go of her hand and moved across the room. Shelley waited just inside, where he'd left her. He struck a match, then touched it to the wick of a lantern. The room filled with a soft glow.

"Doesn't the electricity work?" she asked, as she looked at the way the light played across his nearly naked physique.

"I don't have any. Too expensive to bring it clear over here. This works fine. Usually I go to bed early anyway."

She continued to hover at the door, watching the way the light revealed the mat of thick hair on his chest. It was the same brown as the hair on his head and mustache. Jack's shoulders and arms were fairly muscular, yet he had the trim, lean look of a diver, especially through his waist and hips.

Shelley wasn't the type to drool over the hunks who hung around the beach at Malibu or Santa Monica, but there was something about Jack Kincaid's body that did things to her. Or maybe it was his independent character—his go-it-alone individualism—in combination with his good looks that affected her so much.

When their gazes met, she realized he'd been noticing her looking at him. She hastily glanced away, surveying the room. "It's quite charming," she said. "Not at all what I expected."

"What did you expect?"

"I don't know—something more . . . basic."

He smiled. "It was more basic before Chantal decorated for me. It's not entirely her doing, though. I've added some touches of my own."

"I thought I detected a woman's hand."

"I do my own housekeeping, if that's any compensation," he said.

"That's more than I can say. I loathe housework."

He beckoned her. "Come on in, Shelley. I won't bite."

She smiled at his teasing and moved into the cozy room, thinking she might have gone too far in presuming he intended to seduce her. But she was in a rather vulnerable position—not quite on a deserted island with the guy, but fairly close to it. This was the sort of situation men fantasized about, and she knew it. Even worse, Jack Kincaid was the type of man who ended up with what he wanted. Chantal had said as much.

She paused to run her hand over the linen cloth on the table. Then she looked into his eyes, trying to find the right way to relate to him, the proper tone to strike.

He was directly across from her now. He leaned on the back of a chair and peered right at her, waiting for her to make a move.

"Were you expecting Chantal this evening?" she asked. "You mistook me for her."

"I'm not expecting her, but there aren't many people who drop by. She's about the only visitor I ever have."

Shelley didn't have to ask what sort of visits they were. "I hope you weren't too disappointed it was me."

"You put me in an awkward situation, my dear. If I say I'm disappointed, I offend you. If I say I'm glad it was you, I'll be accused of having unsavory intentions."

"It's never a mistake to be honest."

He smiled wryly. "Then I'll admit it. I'm glad it was you."

Blushing, she turned and walked over to the sideboard where Jack had set up her uncle's chess set. She picked up the black king, fingering it. "I think we need a new subject."

"All right. Why don't you have a drink while I grab a quick shower?" he said. "I don't like salt water to dry on me. There's sherry and a couple of kinds of wine in the cabinet below you. Glasses are in there, too." He gestured toward the chess set. "Maybe we can play a game after dinner, in honor of Henry."

"If there's time."

"In this part of the world, Shelley, time is yours to do with as you wish. You have all night." He gave her a sardonic grin and went off to the bedroom.

Shelley stood there for a long moment, thinking. These situations always had a winner and a loser, and she'd be hard-pressed to deny that Jack Kincaid had come out on top this round. Dinner, a game of chess, then time to do whatever she wished. The guy was as masterful as she was foolish.

She took a glass from the cupboard, poured herself some sherry, and sat down to wait for Jack Kincaid to have his shower.

BEFORE HE RETURNED, Shelley succumbed to her curiosity and inspected the room more closely. The paintings, mostly landscapes, were signed "Chantal." The style was the same as those she'd seen at Chantal's house, but she hadn't noticed the signature there. So Chantal was a painter, too.

Jack's bookcase proved to have quite a variety of reading material. There were a few books on aviation and sailing, but the rest were on history, philosophy, art and poetry. There were biographies of strong, independent-minded men like Napoleon, Jefferson, MacArthur, but also the writings of freethinkers like Emerson and Thoreau. The fiction section contained the work of John Fowles, E. L. Doctorow, Joyce Carol Oates, Ernest Hemingway and Heinrich Böll. The Hemingway didn't surprise her; the rest did.

She was at the bookcase when he came out. She glanced over her shoulder at him. "You must read these. They couldn't be here just to impress your visitors, since you never have any."

"True. And I do read them."

Shelley turned to face him. Wet and slicked back, his hair was much darker. Together with the mustache, it gave him an old-fashioned air. He had on a faded light-blue work shirt, khaki shorts and sandals.

Jack went to the sideboard and poured himself a sherry. He held up the bottle, offering her another, but she shook her head. Then he sauntered over to the bookcase and touched his glass to hers.

"*Salut*." He sipped the wine, giving her a quirky grin.

Shelley got a big whiff of his tangy cologne. It was an unusual fragrance and she liked it. She took a tiny sip from her glass. "So you're a closet intellectual."

"No, but I enjoy reading. TV reception's not too good around here, you see."

She smiled. "And kind of hard to find a place to plug in the set?"

"Yeah, that too."

They looked into each other's eyes. Then Jack took her by the arm. "Come on, we might as well sit down and enjoy our drink before I start dinner."

Shelley went with him to the love seat. They sat very close to each other, but not quite touching. Jack crossed his legs. She fiddled with the top button of her shirt, remembering the haste in which she'd dressed.

"You're an unusual person," she said, feeling the need to fill the silence. "I'm still having trouble figuring out why you're living here. It can't be because of a lousy marriage."

Jack took a sip of sherry. "It's not, really. A bad marriage will wake you up, make you ask questions you otherwise wouldn't, but no, it shouldn't send anyone into seclusion."

"Then why *are* you here?"

"Because I like it, Shelley. I like the quiet. I like the beauty. I can do what I want here and not worry about anyone or anything."

"Isn't that a little selfish?"

"Maybe, but so what? Ninety percent of the rest of the world is climbing up somebody else's back. Not being a saint, I do the next best thing to devoting myself to humanity—I disengage."

"Well, if you don't get lonely living like this, you must be pretty strong."

He grinned. "I'm not a hermit, so I'm not so sure strength has anything to do with it."

It suddenly seemed important to know everything she could about Jack Kincaid. "Why didn't you marry Chantal?"

He gave her a look. "Our relationship really interests you, doesn't it?"

"I'm sorry if I was prying."

"Oh, I don't mind. It just strikes me as funny."

"Well, her paintings are on your wall. She's the only one who comes here. You were lovers at some point, obviously. And you seem well matched. I'm curious why—that is, it seems you're well suited for each other.... She *is* lovely."

"Some things aren't easily explained."

"You clearly don't hate each other," she continued. "I mean, you aren't enemies."

"No."

"Is it because she wants to develop the island and you don't?"

Jack looked at her.

Shelley put her hand to her mouth. "Oops."

"That's all right. I already assumed she's been talking to you about turning this place into a resort. Her desires are no secret. And she would be foolish not to try."

"Is that what's come between you?"

"No. We had a relationship—a good one in many respects—but it only went so far. Relationships do that sometimes—just stop, and you know it's over. Ours did and we remained friends—our differences over the future of the island notwithstanding.

"Frankly, I regard Chantal's plans as a pipe dream. But if they work out for her, I'll probably stick around for a while and see how things go. Should I not like what I see, I'll move on."

"Kincaid, you're just a cowboy, you know that? You drift."

He smiled broadly. "You say that with such admiration."

She gave him a jab with her elbow. "I'm not used to guys like you, that's all."

Jack patted her thigh in a friendly sort of way. It was overly familiar, but she wasn't alarmed. Then he rested his hand on her leg for a moment, which did get her attention. "Better get used to me, kiddo. I may be a cowboy, but for the next several days, I'm all you've got." With that he got to his feet and peered down at her with the doggonedest sexy look she'd ever seen. "Guess I'd better play the good host and feed you," he said, his lips curling under his mustache. "Getting hungry?"

She stared at his mouth, speculating what it would be like to kiss him. "Yeah, I could eat."

"Want to help, or do you prefer to play lady of leisure?"

"I'll help."

"Like to peel potatoes?"

"I adore peeling potatoes."

Jack offered her his hand, pulling her to her feet. He didn't let go of her hand right away. Shelley gazed up at him, feeling the vibrations stronger than ever.

Suddenly she remembered. "Oh, my God. Uncle Henry's journals! I left them outside." She went to the front door. The case was sitting where she'd left it. Jack came up behind her. "It's still here, thank goodness."

"There's no place for a suitcase to go on this island."

"Maybe so, but I lugged it all the way down here. Of course, that was when I thought Claude was a burglar."

"Well, no point leaving it outside," Jack said, picking it up. He carried it in and put it in the corner. "That thing is heavy. I'm amazed you could get it all the way down here."

"I'm stronger than I look."

Jack let his gaze skitter down her bare legs, making no attempt to hide his obvious admiration. "You're fairly unusual yourself, Shelley. Definitely not your average city girl."

"Why do you say that?"

"I don't know. Just a feeling I have." He winked and headed for the tiny kitchen. "Come on, let's rustle up some grub."

JACK STOOD AT THE butane stove, stirring the vegetables. He glanced over at Shelley, who was bending over, picking up a couple of chips of potato peel. She had fantastic legs and a nice round little derriere that certainly hadn't gone unnoticed. When she turned, she caught him looking at her and she smiled. He gave a half shrug, which brought an admonishing frown from her.

"Considering how few visitors you have," she said, with a touch of sarcasm, "the appropriate attire for a female guest is probably a nun's habit."

"I'm accountable for what I do, not for what I think."

"Well, kindly keep your thoughts to yourself."

He put down the wooden stirring spoon, took a pinch of salt and sprinkled it into the potatoes. "When I first saw you on the sidewalk outside Mabel's office, I knew you'd be a handful. But I had no idea how much, to be perfectly honest."

Shelley put her hands on her hips. "What's that supposed to mean?"

He leaned against the counter, folding his arms over his chest. "I was just commenting on the friendly hostility that seems to be dogging our relationship."

"What friendly hostility?"

"Don't you notice the tension that flares between us at the least little thing?"

"That's the natural opposition of the sexes," she replied. "You shouldn't take it personally."

"Why is it I don't notice the same thing with other women?"

Shelley shrugged innocently. "Maybe they aren't as intractable as I am. And you probably haven't worked for many of them, either. Not all men are comfortable being accountable to a woman, you know."

Jack smiled at her, amused by their jousting. "In other words, the problem is with *my* ego, not yours."

"Perhaps we'd be better off worrying about fixing dinner than trying to decide whose ego does what. Where are the dishes? I'll set the table."

"In the cabinet next to the sink."

He put the sauté pan on the burner, glancing over at Shelley, who was up on her toes, reaching for the plates on the upper shelf. "If you come over often, I'll have to lower the cabinets," he said, as he stepped over to help her.

"No short jokes, Kincaid. Being below average in size just means I have a compact punch."

He chuckled. "How often have you used that line?"

"I believe it's a first," she said, poking her tongue in her cheek.

"You know," he said, tweaking her chin, "it's amazing how much we have in common."

"You're incorrigible," she said, taking the plates from him. "Better mind your cooking." With that, she left the room.

Jack returned to the stove, smiling to himself. He was having a good time. Shelley Van Dam was not only cute—quite attractive, actually—but she was also fun to spar with.

And she had gotten that natural-opposition-of-the-sexes business right. His hormones were humming and that wasn't necessarily good—not if she really wanted to play this thing straight.

After leaving her that morning, he'd decided to cool the attraction he'd felt right from the beginning. It wasn't worth the trouble. But now that he'd seen her in those shorts, his natural instincts came to the fore again—despite the fact that she did seem to be fairly serious about discouraging him.

Shelley came back to the kitchen. "Where's the silverware?"

"That drawer there," he said, pointing.

She took what she needed and was gone again. Jack put the fish he'd prepared into the pan and watched it sizzle, all the while thinking about Shelley. She'd commented on him being different, but *she* was, too. In fact, he couldn't recall running across a woman quite like her.

Usually his relationships were pretty straightforward. He tended to make clear what he wanted and he had a knack for getting the lady in question to want the same thing. Usually they had the same thing in mind anyway, and that was that. Of course, he and women like Shelley Van Dam didn't frequently cross trails, so this was not a normal situation.

"What are we drinking, Jack?" she called from the other room.

"Feel like some wine? I picked up a couple of bottles of sauterne recently. They're a step up from *vin de table*, but nothing fancy."

She came to the kitchen door. "I wouldn't mind a glass, but that's all. So don't open a bottle for me."

"What the heck. It'll keep. But I've got to watch the fish, so if you don't mind getting a bottle and the opener, I'll uncork it. Wine's in the buffet." He glanced at her leaning against the doorframe, an appraising look on her face.

"Just a small glass. That's all I'm having."

"Roger. I read."

Her lips reluctantly curled into a smile and she turned and walked off. Jack watched her, sighing. Maybe this living-alone business was more self-denying than he'd realized.

A few minutes later the food was on the table. They sat across from each other, a single candle between them. One of the lanterns was on the sideboard, casting a warm glow throughout the room.

Jack picked up his glass. *"Bon appétit!"*

Shelley returned his salute.

"Nice to have a dinner guest," he said, eyeing her over the flickering candle.

"I appreciate your hospitality under what I know are difficult circumstances."

"What do you mean?" he asked. "The natural opposition of the sexes?"

"I'll probably live to regret that term," she said, sipping her wine. "What I meant was, I'm well aware that by coming here and staying for dinner I'm giving a signal that could easily be misinterpreted."

"Shelley, Shelley, that problem's been laid to rest. Just enjoy your dinner. Don't drink too much. I might challenge you to a game of chess after dessert."

She picked up her knife and fork, taking a bite of fish. "Ah, delicious."

"Glad you like it."

They ate in silence then.

"Jack," she said after several minutes, "there's something I want to tell you."

"Yes?"

"I've made arrangements to dispose of Uncle Henry's notebooks and his other research materials."

Business. That's what had been on her mind. He was surprised at how disappointed he was. "Oh yeah, when did this happen?"

"This afternoon. I called France from Chantal's."

He nodded, chewing his food. "All right."

"I wasn't going to discuss it with you because... frankly, I'm confused about what's going on."

"And you weren't sure if you could trust me."

"Well, I wouldn't put it that way."

"No need for false diplomacy," he said. "I'm a big boy."

"The truth is, I'm aware I need someone I can trust. I'd like for it to be you."

"I was sort of under the impression we were already at that point."

"I thought so, too."

Something was bothering her. "You're not so sure?"

Her expression became anxious. "Please be honest with me, Jack. Were you really the one who mailed the journals to me?"

"Yes, but if I hadn't been and I was up to no good, I'd lie about it. So it doesn't matter much what I say."

"I'm a pretty good judge of character," she said, looking him in the eye. "I just wanted to hear you say it. I can tell a lot about people that way."

Jack wiped his mouth with his napkin. "Now that is scary."

Shelley laughed. "You can also tell a lot about people by the way they play chess. My father taught me that," she said.

"Maybe I should reconsider my challenge." He picked up the bottle of wine, reached across the table and poured more into her glass.

"I thought you said not to drink too much," she reminded, lifting the neck of the bottle to stop him from pouring.

He winked. "That was before I discovered you're seriously into gamesmanship."

She picked up her glass, and held it to her lips. "Thanks, Jack."

"For what?"

"For not asking who I was giving the journals to. I wanted you not to care."

He shrugged. "I might as well be honest with you. I already know it's Philippe Dufour."

She looked surprised. "How did you know that?"

"You said you called France. There couldn't have been too many choices."

She slowly nodded. "You're a lot more complicated than I thought. I've got to be careful with you, don't I?"

"Yes, my dear," he replied. "You certainly do."

6

SHELLEY LOOKED AT HER king, hopelessly surrounded, her own pieces helpless to defend him. She glanced up at Jack, whose face was impassive. That annoyed her.

"Doesn't look very promising for the good guys," she said.

"Unless I'm mistaken, it's mate in three moves."

She took her king and gently laid him on his side. "I'll take your word for it. I resign."

"Do you want me to show you the moves?"

"Thanks. I can see I'm beaten."

"You put up a spirited fight."

"Don't patronize me, Jack. You trounced me twice."

"You did play much better the second game," he insisted.

"Don't worry, I'll play you again and again—however long it takes to beat you," she said. "I'm not a very good loser."

Jack fingered his empty wineglass, then leaned back in his chair, folding his arms over his chest.

They were at the table. Shelley sat back, too. She folded her arms, parroting him. They exchanged long looks.

"Please take this in the honorable spirit in which it's offered," Jack began. "I think you should spend the night here. Henry's place will seem like a tomb and it's pointless going back there until morning. You can have my bed if you don't like the idea of the couch. I can always sleep out here."

By all rights she should say no. Sending the wrong signal would be the worst possible thing to do. But Shelley was weary, and deep down she knew he was right—the plantation house would seem like a tomb. She would just have to hope that Jack would understand her motives and not misinterpret her acceptance. "Okay, fine," she said. "So long as we understand each other."

He stifled a yawn. "We do."

Shelley felt better. She'd worried all evening about going back, but the notion of staying had worried her, too. "I appreciate your attitude. A lot of men would try and take advantage of the situation."

"I'm not a sex maniac."

"That's reassuring," she said with a laugh.

He was watching her again, the expression on his face almost admiring. "What'll it be, the bedroom or the sofa?"

"I'll sleep out here. There's no reason to chase you out of your bed on top of everything else." She stood, stretching her tired body, stifling a yawn herself. "This has been a long day."

Jack got to his feet. "Yeah, ditto." He smiled across the table in a collegial way. "I'll get some bedding."

"A blanket and a pillow are all I need."

"Sure?"

"Positive."

"Use the bathroom first, if you like," he said, pointing to the bedroom door. "Here—" he lifted the candle from the sideboard "—take this, so you'll have light."

Shelley went off to the bathroom, noticing, as she passed through the tiny bedroom, that it was as neat as the rest of the cottage.

When she came back to the main room, Jack had gotten the bedding. He set the lantern on the end table next to the sofa.

"You can turn this off when you're ready to go to sleep."

"Thanks, Jack," she said.

He took her by the shoulders and lightly kissed her on the cheek. "Good night, kiddo."

It was a bit presumptuous, but Shelley didn't mind—not if he kept his word about being a gentleman. "Good night, Jack."

Taking the candle he disappeared into the bedroom, closing the door behind him. Shelley sat down heavily on the sofa. Although she was exhausted, she felt good about the evening despite the flare-ups between them. Her gaze fell on the suitcase filled with Henry's journals. She was reasonably confident Jack could be trusted. At least, she hoped so. She'd pretty well put everything, including herself, in his hands, so he'd better be as decent as he professed to be.

She fluffed the pillow, lay down and spread the blanket over her legs. Despite the proximity of the sea and the open windows and doors, the air remained pleasantly balmy. If memory served, it would cool some during the small hours, but it wouldn't get cold.

She reached back, turning down the lantern until the room was plunged into darkness. Through the open doors and windows she could see the night sky and the moon. With everything so quiet, she could hear the sea swelling up and splashing against the rocks somewhere below. It was a soothing sound.

As she lay there, Shelley realized how seemingly idyllic Jack Kincaid's life was. Of course, it was unreal, too—just as cowboys and flyboys and other adventurers were unreal. She had to hand it to him, though. He was doing what he wanted.

Still, she thought he led a rather selfish life. Modern living could be pretty difficult, but it didn't seem right to her that a person should run from it. She thought of her own work, feeling good about what she did.

Shelley closed her eyes and pictured her condo in Santa Monica. It was a comfortable place, though hardly ostentatious by West L.A. standards. She thought of the night before she'd left to fly to the Caribbean. Warren had come over for a drink, to say goodbye. They'd sat on her big overstuffed cream sofa and talked about their work.

Warren had been laboring over a deal between a production company and one of the bigger studios. He'd had an important and successful meeting that day. She'd been interested in hearing his account of it because his work often put him in contact with powerful people—sometimes even celebrities.

And yet, when she thought of their last evening together, she thought of the smell of tobacco smoke on his clothes, the expression on his face when she'd brought him a second drink and his mind had made the shift from business to her. Warren had put his hand on her knee and, even though she'd half expected that they would end up in bed, it had struck her that she didn't want to make love with him. Just because they'd had two drinks, and just because it would be two weeks before they had another opportunity, was no reason that it had to happen.

Warren hadn't been angry when she told him she wasn't in the mood for sex. He'd taken it in stride, as any decent man would. He'd kissed her goodbye and Shelley had gone to bed thinking that he was the kind of man she wanted, and that that was the way things ought to be.

But now, thousands of miles from Los Angeles, she had to admit that Warren wasn't what she wanted—not really. Everything had changed—in the course of a single day. And it wasn't too difficult to figure out the reason.

She glanced at Jack's bedroom door. Like Warren, he had behaved like a gentleman. He hadn't forced himself on her. But the difference was that Jack had made her think she would have liked it if he had.

Shelley closed her eyes and pictured his door slowly opening. His face would be lit by a single candle. He would be bare-chested and there would be a smile curving under his mustache as he made his way to the couch. Then he would sit down next to her, put his hand to her face, and insist he couldn't sleep until he'd kissed her properly.

And when his lips touched hers, she would kiss him back. His hand would find its way under her shirt and soon he'd have her naked and wanting him. They would make love, and in the morning they'd both behave as though nothing had happened. She would finish her business on Saint Maurice and then go home. Jack would have had his fantasy, and she'd have had hers.

And once she was back in Los Angeles, she would end things with Warren. The next man she made love with would be capable of coming to her with a candle and making love by the light of its flickering flame. The next man in her life would be a lot more like Jack Kincaid.

JACK'S VOICE AWAKENED her. "We've got visitors, Shelley," he called from the kitchen. "You might want to get up."

Her eyes blinked open. "Visitors?" she echoed, sleepily.

Jack came into the front room and walked past her to the window. "It's Chantal, and she's got somebody with her."

Shelley could hear the sound of the Jeep now. She sat bolt upright. "Lord, I've got to get up." She scrambled to her feet and started folding the blanket.

"Here, I'll take care of that," Jack said, coming over. "You go to the bathroom if you want."

Grateful for his consideration, she went off. A few minutes of refuge was exactly what she needed. The face looking back at her in the mirror was puffy, her pale hair a tangled mess. "Lord," she mumbled. She didn't even have a comb with her, so she ran her fingers through her mop, making it as presentable as she could.

She eyed Jack's tube of toothpaste lying beside the basin. She didn't have a brush, but her finger would do in an emergency, and this qualified. She did the best she could and, as she was rinsing her mouth, she heard voices in the other room. Groaning, she smoothed her clothes and headed for the front room, realizing how bad it looked to be coming out of Jack's bedroom first thing in the morning.

"Bonjour," Chantal said upon seeing her. A knowing smile appeared at the corners of her mouth. Chantal was standing in the middle of the room with Jack and another man.

"Good morning."

"I'm glad you took my advice and didn't stay by yourself last night," Chantal gently chided.

Jack was grinning from ear to ear. Shelley could have killed him. Why didn't he explain?

"Well, Shelley, I've brought you a visitor," Chantal announced. "This is Karl Baumann. He's come all the way from Germany to see you."

Shelley's eyes went back to the stranger. Baumann was sixtyish, stocky, with a ruddy complexion and was wearing a gray suit.

"Good morning, Mrs. Van Dam," he said, his accent so thick he sounded like a parody of a German businessman. "I have indeed come all the way from Europe, especially to see you."

Shelley made her way over to him. Baumann extended his hand and, as he shook hers, he clicked his heels slightly. Shelley had to restrain herself from smiling.

"We haven't met before, have we, Mr. Baumann?"

"No, indeed, Mrs. Van Dam. I was acquainted with your late uncle, however. We have done business in the past and it is business I come to discuss with you now."

"I see."

"Mr. Baumann arrived by boat and insisted I take him to the plantation house immediately," Chantal explained. "When we didn't find you home, I assumed you would be here."

"I had an intruder last evening," Shelley explained. "He frightened me to death so I came here for safety. It turned out to be a false alarm."

"Claude scared the devil out of her," Jack added. "She didn't know who he was."

Shelley was grateful for the support, and acknowledged it with a nod. Chantal, apparently unconvinced, still wore her little smile. She wasn't being unkind, exactly, but Shelley felt compelled to clarify any misapprehension just the same. "I slept on the sofa," she declared. "By myself."

"Yes," Jack added. "And I slept in the bedroom, as usual."

Chantal chuckled. "We are not the police, after all."

"You see—" Jack turned to Shelley "—Chantal's a very liberal-minded woman."

Shelley gave him a look.

"Anyway," Chantal interjected, "I believe Mr. Baumann has something important to discuss."

"Yes, Mrs. Van Dam," he said, taking the cue, "I would like to talk with you, please."

"Chantal and I can go out on the veranda," Jack volunteered. "I've made some coffee. Can I get anyone a cup?"

Baumann and Shelley declined.

"How about you, Chantal?" Jack asked. "Care to join me?"

"Gladly," she said. *"Merci."*

They disappeared into the kitchen and Shelley and Karl Baumann sat down at the table. The businessman mumbled pleasantries while removing some papers from his inside pocket. Shelley hardly paid any attention to him, listening instead to Jack and Chantal, who were laughing in the kitchen. They soon went out to the patio where Jack pulled two chairs together and they sat side by side in the morning sun.

"I know you Americans like to get to the matter directly," Baumann said, "so I will tell you why I am here."

"I would appreciate that."

"I am a representative of Deitz-Langen S.A., Mrs. Van Dam. We are the largest pharmaceutical company in Europe, if you do not know the name. Our researchers are familiar with the work of your late uncle, and find his results most important. We believe that such a significant body of work should be preserved and used for the benefit of all society. Therefore we are prepared to purchase his scientific research for an excellent price."

Shelley was taken completely by surprise. "I had no idea Uncle Henry's work was so highly regarded."

"There is much to be learned from Herr Professor Van Dam's excellent methods. We are hopeful you will entrust Deitz-Langen with this important responsibility."

Out on the terrace Chantal laughed and said to Jack, *"Tu blague, chéri."* Shelley wasn't sure what the words meant, and couldn't hear anything else, but it was pretty evident they were having a good time. She wondered if the cause of the amusement was a joke at her expense.

"I have come to inquire about your terms, Mrs. Van Dam," the German said. "Let me only say that we will purchase the research separately, or if you prefer, we will purchase your uncle's entire estate, including all the land he owns on the island."

"I very much appreciate your interest, Mr. Baumann, but I'm afraid arrangements for my uncle's research have already been made."

"What's this?" he asked with dismay.

"The decision was not mine. It was made for me," Shelley explained. "My uncle left instructions about the disposition of his work, and I am duty-bound to follow it."

"Are you sure? I have no knowledge of this."

"I didn't either, before arriving at Saint Maurice. I have instructions and I plan to follow them to the letter." Shelley's gaze moved to Jack and Chantal, whom she could see just over the German's shoulder. Chantal was laughing about something and patting Jack's cheek. Shelley found the display of affection annoying.

"If it is a question of money," Baumann said, "I am prepared to offer you an attractive price. Five million dollars, U.S., for everything. Would that interest you, Mrs. Van Dam?"

"Five million?"

"Yes. Or if you prefer, a million for the research alone." He hesitated. "Make it two million."

"My," she replied, "you certainly are eager."

The man's florid face turned dour. "I explained how important we regard this matter."

"Yes, you did," Shelley said, as she watched Chantal stroll toward the cliff, her dark hair and her dress blowing in the breeze. She cut a rather romantic figure and Shelley found that she begrudgingly admired her. How could Jack not be attracted to her?

Baumann, seeing her distraction, turned around to see what she was looking at.

"I'm sorry, forgive me," Shelley said. "What I'm trying to say is that it's not a matter of money. I have no choice."

He appeared glum. "This is most disappointing, Mrs. Van Dam."

"I'm sorry you came all the way from Europe for nothing."

"When I heard you were on Saint Maurice, I came right away," he explained.

Shelley pondered the comment. "Tell me, how did you know I was here?"

"Why, Madame Favre informed me by telephone."

"Chantal?" Shelley's gaze returned to Chantal, who was making her way back to the terrace.

"Since she is in authority, when we heard of your uncle's death, we requested to be notified when the heir arrived. I assume there is no problem in this," Baumann said.

"No, of course not."

The German drummed his fingers on the table. "Would it be improper to inquire who will be the beneficiary of Herr Professor Van Dam's research?"

"A number of things are still up in the air," she replied. "I think it is premature to disclose that."

"I understand," Baumann replied, looking displeased. "Well, I will not take more of your time." Placing a business card in front of her, he said, "If there is a change in the situation, you will call me?"

"Yes, certainly."

With that, Karl Baumann got to his feet. "Delightful woman, Madame Favre," he remarked.

"Yes," Shelley agreed. "Chantal is quite lovely."

Shelley went to the doorway accessing the terrace. "Mr. Baumann is ready to go, Chantal," she said.

"Already?" She and Jack came back inside. She glanced back and forth between Shelley and the businessman. "It went well?"

"I'm afraid not," Baumann answered. "Mrs. Van Dam has other commitments."

A brief wave of disappointment passed over Chantal's face before it was quickly replaced with a polite smile. "Well, you can enjoy our climate and the sea for a few days, Mr. Baumann, *n'est-ce pas?*"

"I'm afraid not, Madame Favre. I must return to Germany." Baumann stiffly shook Shelley's hand, then Jack's, and marched directly out the door to the Jeep.

Chantal paused a minute before going after him. "Well, now you can have your breakfast in peace." She smiled. *"Bon appétit."* Swishing her skirt, she went to the door where she stopped. "Oh, by the way, the gendarmes will be arriving from Saint Barts soon. Shall I take them to the plantation house or here?"

"To Uncle Henry's, please," Shelley said. "That's where I intend to spend *all* my time."

Chantal managed to keep a straight face as she went off.

Shelley gave Jack a woebegone look. "Well, have we scandalized the island?"

"To the contrary, Chantal thinks we make a cute couple."

"Did she say that?"

He chortled. "Not in so many words. That's the gist of it."

"Presumably you straightened her out," she said.

"About what?"

"About us. We aren't a cute couple. I mean, we aren't *any* kind of couple."

"Don't get so excited, Shelley. I told her all we did was play chess."

"And what did she say?"

"She just laughed."

"Oh, Jack, you're impossible."

Then Jack plucked at Shelley's curls with his fingers and put an arm around her shoulders. "So tell me, Raggedy Ann, how do you like your eggs?"

DURING BREAKFAST SHELLEY told him about Karl Baumann's offer, and she was thinking about it as he walked her back to the house.

"Uncle Henry must have been involved in something big," she said. "Five million bucks is a lot of money."

"That included the house and the land, right?"

"Yes. Strange, isn't it? What would a pharmaceutical company want with property on this island?"

"Baumann might have a nose for real estate. Or he might have talked to Chantal."

"She was the one who called him and told him I was here."

"Oh?"

"Do you think she's in cahoots with them?"

"She didn't say anything to me," he replied. "But it wouldn't be like her to pass up an opportunity."

Shelley thought for a moment. "By the way, what were the two of you laughing about out on the terrace?"

"You don't want to know."

"Yes, I do."

He gave her a skeptical look. "Chantal wanted to know if I was going to marry you to make sure Saint Maurice remained unchanged."

Shelley rolled her eyes. "That *is* funny."

"I thought so."

"You see, Jack, I never should have stayed the night at your place. I guess I was thinking I was still in the city, where nobody cares."

"Do *you* care?" he asked.

"I know it was innocent."

"Then the hell with everybody else."

She gave him an ironic grin. "That pretty well sums up your philosophy, doesn't it?"

He smiled. "You know, Chantal was right. We do make a cute couple."

Shelley was so annoyed that she began walking faster and faster, leaving Jack behind. Yet a part of her really enjoyed their bantering, or at least was amused by it. She wasn't used to playfulness in a man and she rather liked it. When she got several yards ahead of him, she stopped and waited, putting her hands on her hips. He finally sauntered up to her.

"You're still having trouble with the pace of things here in the Caribbean, aren't you?" he said.

"Let's just say I'm having trouble with *your* pace of life."

"It won't do any good to whip me. I march at my own speed."

She settled into the same easy gait. "Yes, you warned me about that, didn't you, Jack?"

He put an arm around her shoulders as the plantation house came into sight. "Relax, kiddo. Try to enjoy yourself."

Shelley didn't object to the familiarity, but she doubted it would be possible for her to relax that much. Not considering the problems she was facing—one of which being Jack Kincaid himself.

At first she'd regarded him as an mere annoyance, but since last night he'd been upgraded to the full status of problem—and not entirely for negative reasons. Little by little she was coming to like him. A lot more than circumstances warranted.

When they reached the plantation house Shelley looked around to ensure that everything was as she'd left it, while Jack found some tools and went to work fixing the front door.

He was removing the door from its hinges as she went upstairs to freshen up. While she worked with her hair she thought again about the Deitz-Langen offer and Uncle Henry's comments about not wanting his research to fall into the wrong hands. Could he have meant Deitz-Langen?

Shelley had changed into a peach T-shirt dress and was putting on some mascara when she heard the island Jeep. A few minutes later she came downstairs to find Chantal in the entry hall with two uniformed police officers. Jack was leaning against the doorframe, watching.

The sober faces of the gendarmes told Shelley something was wrong. Gone, too, was Chantal's happy countenance of earlier that morning. She greeted Shelley at the foot of the stairs, then introduced her to the gendarmes.

The older of the two men, Guy Lasserre, was the captain. He was small, but his bearing was ramrod straight. His silvery mustache was trimmed precisely and his khaki uniform was starched and immaculate. He saluted Shelley, put his cap under his arm, and shook her hand.

"I am sorry to meet you under such unfortunate circumstances, *madame*," he said stiffly, "but I'm afraid I have unpleasant news."

"What's that?"

"We have received the results of the autopsy on your uncle, and the indications do not support the original conclusion of an accidental death. Monsieur Van Dam sustained a blow to the head—probably by a sharp wooden object with distinctive ridges. There were no other contusions on the body, which would be expected in a fall down the stairs. In other words, *madame*, we now suspect murder."

"Murder?"

"*Oui, madame.*"

Shelley was shocked. She glanced at Chantal, then at Jack, who remained at the door, his arms folded over his chest. "I can't believe anyone would murder Uncle Henry."

"That is the conclusion of the experts," the captain said. "Of course, there must be an investigation. Our previous inquiry was with a different object in mind. Now we must search for the murderer, the murder weapon, and other evidence of the crime."

"I understand."

"You have no objection, then, if we look around the house?"

"No, none whatsoever."

"We are told by Madame Favre that you have straightened the house since the burglary," the officer said.

"That's correct."

"It is unfortunate since this crime may in some way be connected with the murder. But of course, no one could have known. Nevertheless we shall see what we can find."

"I'll cooperate in any way I can, Captain Lasserre," she said.

"I do have a few questions."

"Yes?"

"Can you tell me, *madame*, has anything been removed from the premises?"

"Well, no, I don't believe so. We've straightened the mess, but everything should still be here. Jack cleaned the laboratory, but I believe everything was dumped in back." She looked over at him. "Isn't that right, Jack?"

He sauntered over to the group. "Yes, Captain, I made a pile of the debris just outside the laboratory door."

"Very good."

"Oh," Shelley interjected, "there'll be one thing missing from the laboratory besides whatever the burglars took. One of my uncle's friends came last night to remove a potted plant that belonged to him."

"A potted plant . . ." the officer repeated. "That probably is not important, but we should talk to him anyway. Who was it?"

"Claude Perrin," Jack said.

"Make a note," Lasserre told his assistant, a boyish-looking officer who appeared to be getting too fat for his uniform. "In due course, I'm sure we will be speaking to all the residents of the island."

"There's one other thing that's been removed," Jack said. "I took Henry's chess set to my home."

"Oh, yes, I forgot about that," Shelley said. "I gave the set to Mr. Kincaid as a gift."

"Perhaps we can examine it when we call on you, Mr. Kincaid," the captain replied.

"Sure. The board is quite heavy. It could do some damage."

"We shall see," the policeman said. "Now *monsieur, mesdames*, if you will excuse us we will begin our inspection."

The two officers went off and Chantal, Jack and Shelley stared at one another.

"I'm very sorry for this," Chantal said. "It's terrible to think someone would kill Monsieur Van Dam. Our island is so peaceful."

"Greed easily turns peace into war," Jack observed.

"What greed?" Chantal asked.

"This morning Mr. Baumann offered me five million dollars for Uncle Henry's property," Shelley said. "That is what you're referring to, Jack, isn't it?"

"It's the most glaring example."

Chantal glanced back and forth between them. "I was aware of this," she said. "In fact, I suggested to Herr Baumann that he might want to offer for the house and land as well as Monsieur Van Dam's research."

"You suggested it?" Shelley countered.

"Yes," Chantal admitted. "I thought one offer to take care of everything might be more appealing to you than finding buyers for each thing. Herr Baumann said his company had no use for the house and land, but I assured him that would be no problem."

"I'll bet you did," Jack said with a laugh.

"Be quiet, scoundrel! At least I do what I can to help. You . . . only make breakfast!"

Jack laughed again and Chantal took a swing at him, but he bounced out of range. Still chuckling, he headed back to the door. "I'll leave you ladies to settle the important matters of state. Me, I'm a humble carpenter."

"He's a villain, that one," Chantal said to Shelley.

"Oh, he is a charmer," Shelley agreed. She saw a hint of regret in Chantal's eyes, but it quickly disappeared.

"What can I do to help you?" Chantal asked her.

"I don't think there's anything. Philippe Dufour hasn't called to say when he's arriving, has he?"

"No. I haven't heard a word from him."

"I had no idea this was going to end up being such a mess," Shelley said to Chantal. "Did Mr. Baumann say anything to you that might explain what's going on?"

"Only that they very much want the research."

"Yes, he made that clear to me, too. Did you mention anything to him about Philippe Dufour?"

Chantal shook her head. "No, Shelley. That is none of my business."

"Don't say anything about it to anyone, okay?"

"Even the police?"

"Well, I suppose they should be informed. If my uncle was murdered, there had to be a reason for it. Several million dollars provides an awful lot of motive."

"Don't say that," Chantal said.

"Why not?"

"Because everything your uncle had is now yours."

"Funny, but I haven't thought of it quite that way."

"Maybe it is best if you get rid of everything and not be bothered," Chantal suggested. "You don't need this trouble."

Shelley studied her for a moment. Why was Chantal so eager to get her out of the picture? Was she simply trying to be helpful, or was it because of her own plans for the property? Or could it be because of Jack? Women often did strange things when they were in love.

"You might be right, Chantal," she said. "Maybe I should sell everything as quickly as I can and get out."

7

"MADAME VAN DAM," Captain Lasserre called from the hallway, "could I have a word with you and Madame Favre?"

Shelley and Chantal silently followed the policeman back into the library where they found his assistant kneeling at the edge of the carpet, examining it.

"There are bloodstains," the captain said. "Both in the rug and on the wood floor. They have been washed, but not completely. The stains are still visible."

The women went over to the spot. Looking closely, Shelley could see a slight discoloration in the carpet.

"We think Monsieur Van Dam may have been murdered here," Lasserre continued. "The killer then carried or dragged the body to the foot of the staircase to make the death seem accidental. Of course, we cannot be sure until there are tests and the blood types compared. Do you know by some chance how long this stain has been here?"

"I have no idea, Captain Lasserre," Shelley said. "I've only been here two days."

Chantal shook her head. "Nor I. Jack may know."

The captain dispatched his assistant to fetch Jack. The man returned with Jack a few minutes later. Jack examined the carpet. "I'm afraid I'm not very observant when it comes to things like this. I never noticed it before, but that doesn't mean it wasn't here."

"Have you been in this room often, Monsieur Kincaid?" the captain asked.

"Yes, quite often. This is where Henry and I usually played chess."

"Then you were friends with Monsieur Van Dam?"

"In some respects we were good friends. I also worked for Henry as his pilot."

The captain contemplated Jack. "We must talk further, Monsieur Kincaid. I understand you live nearby."

"Yes, at the end of the road, on the water."

Lasserre turned toward Chantal. "Since we are so close, *madame*, perhaps we can call on Monsieur Kincaid later today. I should also like to see this chessboard."

"As you wish."

"Is this agreeable, *monsieur?*" the captain asked Jack.

"Yes, fine. I'll be home. As a matter of fact, I was thinking of heading back now." He glanced at Shelley. "I've gotten the hinges back on the door. It'll hold together for a while, but the whole thing should be replaced."

"I appreciate your help. This house is not hard to break into, but I'll sleep more easily knowing I at least have a front door."

Jack nodded. "I'd best be on my way."

"I'll see you out," she said.

They went to the entry hall, passing by the place where Henry's body had been found. Knowing now that her uncle had been murdered, Shelley found it even more unsettling than before to look at the spot.

"This ordeal has changed from unpleasant to gruesome," she remarked with a shiver.

"I know what you mean. Knowing Henry was murdered, I'm getting even more concerned," he admitted, as he followed her through the door and out onto the veranda.

"About what?"

"You."

They stopped at the top of the steps and Shelley regarded him. "You and Chantal both."

"Too much has happened—the burglary, millions of dollars being bandied about, and now this."

"Chantal's solution is to sell everything fast and get the heck out of here. What's yours?"

"This may sound self-serving, but I don't think you should stay in this house. Not alone. I'd offer to stay with you, but it's pointless when we can be at my place. Forgive me, but it's more comfortable there anyway."

"Chantal wants me to leave Saint Maurice, and you want me to move in with you. Is that what I'm hearing?" she asked, in a teasing tone of voice.

His blue eyes twinkled as he stroked his mustache with his finger. "You stayed with me last night and I don't recall hearing any complaints."

"No, you were a gentleman."

"So you have nothing to fear."

"I'm not one to tempt fate, Jack. An emergency is one thing, to virtually live with you is another entirely. I don't think it's a good idea."

"Well, come for dinner and a game of chess anyway. In fact, come on down this afternoon. I was going to do a little snorkeling. You can join me. Ever tried it?"

"I'm not on vacation. And you don't have to entertain me."

"A pleasant distraction would be good for you. Surely you don't work twenty-four hours a day while you're home."

"No," she said, "I don't, though sometimes it seems as if I do." It was already getting warm and the thought of a swim later, when the heat was intense, did have a certain appeal. And if she was honest, she rather liked the notion of spending more time with Jack Kincaid.

But at the same time she acknowledged that their growing friendship could be dangerous. The sexual fantasies she'd been having about him might turn into reality, and that could only lead to troublesome complications. The image of him swimming naked passed through her mind, and Shelley suddenly found it hard to maintain her composure.

"An awful lot has to be done around here," she pointed out. "The cleaning woman's coming. I've to straighten a lot of stuff. And I have to make an appointment to see Uncle Henry's lawyer. When will you be available to fly me over to Saint Barts, by the way?"

"Tomorrow's good. The day after, I've got a charter that's been scheduled for some time. It's only a one-day thing. After that, I'm completely free."

"I want to get things rolling, so I'll try to make the appointment for tomorrow."

He gave her a beguiling look. "Do you think you can squeeze a swim and some chess into your schedule?"

She contemplated him. "You like to give me a bad time about being a mainlander, don't you?"

"There's a time to be responsible and there's a time to follow one's whims," he said. "Successful living is knowing when to do which."

"You have got to be the world's champion rationalizer, Jack Kincaid."

He grinned. "Bring your suit and an overnight case. Then tonight, after I've thrashed you at chess again, you can decide how responsible you wish to be."

"You're pretty damned cocksure of yourself, aren't you?"

He pinched her cheek. "No, Shelley, I just know how to live." With that he descended the steps and headed for his cottage.

Simone Roche, a stout, large-boned woman of fifty-five, arrived at the plantation house wearing a long skirt, cotton blouse, apron and a large straw hat to protect her from the sun. Chantal introduced Simone to Shelley. They quickly agreed on the work Simone was to do, as well as the wage she would be paid.

When Captain Lasserre learned that Simone had previously worked for Henry, he took the woman into the library and asked whether she had ever before seen the stain in the carpet. Simone assured him that the mark was new, otherwise she would have noticed it previously.

"My theory may be correct," the captain told Shelley and Chantal, who were standing at the entrance to the room. "We will send samples to the crime laboratory." He steepled his fingers, a self-satisfied smile on his face. "And now, *mesdames*, perhaps you would be good enough to leave me and Madame Roche, so that I may question her further."

Shelley and Chantal took the opportunity to drive to the village so that Shelley could call Monsieur Voirin on Saint Barts to arrange an appointment. After climbing into the Jeep, Chantal stared at the crumbling facade of the plantation house, a forlorn expression on her face. "This is very sad when you think about it," she said. "It could be so lovely here."

"One way or the other, it will be again," Shelley replied. "Whether by my efforts or a new owner's."

"Are you considering keeping the property?"

"I really don't know what I'll do."

"*Tiens!*" Chantal exclaimed. "What would you think if we were to be partners? I could run the hotel and you would have to do nothing but take your share of the profits. It would be very good for you!"

"Chantal, you are definitely a businesswoman. I'm surprised you've stayed on Saint Maurice so long. There's lots of money to be made out in the world by someone with your energy and ambition."

Chantal started the Jeep and they headed off. "You are right," she said. "I discovered this myself not so very long ago. I woke up and said, 'Chantal, you are thirty-five. Too much of your life is gone. You must do something now.'" She smiled at Shelley. "And that is what I am doing."

"Did you offer Karl Baumann the same deal you offered me—you will run the hotel and send Deitz-Langen its share of the profits?"

Chantal gave her a wary look. "You are offended."

They were going too fast, as usual, and Shelley had to hang on to keep from bouncing out of the seat. "I'm not offended, I'm just trying to understand you."

"There is nothing to understand, I simply— Ayee!" Chantal screamed as the Jeep skidded to a halt, nearly throwing Shelley through the windshield.

Standing three feet from the bumper was Claude Perrin, his eyes wide with fear. His mouth was open and his tragically disfigured face looked horrified as he dove off the trail, then disappeared into the jungle.

Chantal jumped up on the seat. *"Imbécile!"* she shouted. "I nearly killed you!" Then she dropped back down, clutching the steering wheel. "I don't know what I shout at him for. He cannot hear."

Shelley thought the real problem was the way Chantal drove, but she didn't say anything. They started out again, and by the time they reached Chantal's, they'd both pretty well recovered from the fright.

Chantal telephoned Saint Barts and was able to get Monsieur Voirin at his office. She put Shelley on.

"Madame Van Dam," the lawyer said, "I am so happy to hear from you. We have many urgent matters to discuss."

"Yes, I know. I'm eager to get my uncle's affairs settled. But I've already found a home for the most difficult part—his research."

"Truly?"

"I'll explain when I see you."

They made arrangements to meet the next afternoon at the lawyer's office on Saint Barts.

"A question before you go, *madame*," Voirin said. "You say you've found a home for Henry's research. I hope it doesn't involve Deitz-Langen, the German pharmaceutical firm."

"No, Monsieur Voirin, it doesn't. Why do you ask?"

"This, too, we must discuss tomorrow. It is not a subject for long-distance discussion."

"Very well. See you tomorrow." Shelley hung up, feeling even more unnerved and confused than previously.

Chantal was sitting on the sofa, watching her. "Shelley," she said, "this situation is getting very complicated. I am afraid for you."

By THE TIME THE WOMEN returned to the plantation house the police were ready to leave. Shelley knew it was important to keep the authorities fully informed, so she asked to speak with Captain Lasserre in private. They went into the sitting room where she proceeded to tell the officer everything that had happened since her arrival—the note from her uncle that Chantal had delivered, her conversation with Philippe Dufour, the journals she'd transported from Los Angeles, the fact that she'd carried them to Jack's, Karl Baumann's visit and the warning the lawyer, Monsieur Voirin, had given her about Deitz-Langen.

"I am pleased that you've told me these things, *madame*," Lasserre said, fingering the brim of his kepi, which he balanced carefully on his knee. "I will be broadening my investigation."

"I'm not making any accusations, you understand," Shelley said quickly.

"Of course not," the officer replied. "I appreciate your position. And, if you will allow, *madame*, I have a suggestion."

"Yes?"

"The journals of Monsieur Van Dam should not be left in the possession of Monsieur Kincaid. I cannot say at this moment that they are evidence in the case, but they may contain clues to the crime. I propose that you place them in my custody for safekeeping."

"You aren't suggesting that Jack is involved in Uncle Henry's death, are you?"

"I suggest nothing of the kind. But neither am I prepared to eliminate any potential suspects, *madame*. As of this moment, everyone must be considered a suspect."

"I understand. Are you saying I can't turn over Uncle Henry's notebooks to Professor Dufour, as my uncle wanted me to do?"

The officer thought for a moment. "When will Dufour be arriving?"

"I would think any day now."

"He will come to Saint Barts on his way?"

"Most likely."

"Then perhaps he can examine the journals at the gendarmerie. I would, in any case, be interested in his views on the relevance of the contents."

"Okay, fine. I'll arrange it."

"My thanks, *madame*. Then I have your permission to take Monsieur Van Dam's journals?"

Shelley didn't like the idea of letting go of the notebooks after all the trouble she'd been through over them,
but at least they would be in the hands of the authorities.
"Yes, Captain Lasserre, they're all yours."

"Very good." The man smiled. "And now, I think we
should be on our way. We have many people yet to inter-
view." He rose to his feet and so did Shelley. He offered her
his hand. "Good-day, *madame*."

Simone Roche was on her hands and knees, scrubbing
the tile floor in the entry hall, when they trooped outside
to the Jeep. The boyish-looking policeman climbed in
back, pulling his uniform jacket down over his stomach.
Lasserre, his kepi sitting smartly on his head, saluted
Shelley, who stood on the veranda.

"*Au revoir, madame,*" he said, and climbed into the Jeep
next to Chantal.

She waved at Shelley. "See you later!"

Chantal drove off in the direction of Jack's place. Shelley went back inside, hoping that Jack wouldn't take it
personally that she'd agreed to turn the notebooks over to
Captain Lasserre.

She stopped for a word with Simone. "I appreciate you
doing this, Simone."

"I could have three more to help," the woman said in
broken English. "But for good money one always works,
n'est-ce pas?"

"How long will it take to finish everything?"

"Another day. Perhaps two. Jacques comes tomorrow
for repairs."

"If I'm not here, you can tell him all that I want done."

"*Oui, madame.*"

Did she dare say what was on her mind? But then, it was
no time to be a coward. "Do you know Jack Kincaid very
well?" she asked.

Simone smiled. "He is *beau*, that one."

Shelley nodded. "Do the people here like him?"

"He is . . . how do you say? . . . quiet. But also *sympathique*, *n'est-ce pas?*"

"Yes, Jack's nice."

"Many thought he and Chantal would marry, but not now."

"Why? What happened?"

Simone shrugged. "Who knows? Maybe she wanted to marry Monsieur Van Dam instead. One never knows."

Uncle Henry and Chantal? Shelley was shocked by the very notion. Could Chantal really have been after him? Somehow that didn't seem possible. On the other hand, Chantal did want to turn the old plantation into a resort very badly. Perhaps she'd gotten it into her head to use the old boy to get what she wanted. If so, why hadn't Jack said something to her about it? He surely would have been aware of it.

"I am not one to gossip," Simone said.

Shelley shook her head. "It's none of my affair, so it doesn't matter. Anyway, my uncle is dead."

"That's true," the woman said, crossing herself. "*Tragique.*"

Shelley went upstairs with the idea of cleaning her uncle's room. But first she finished unpacking her own things, a job she'd never completed. She wasn't even sure she'd be staying at the big house that night, considering she planned to take Jack up on his offer.

The day's events had given her pause. It might have been her own paranoia, but everyone seemed tainted with suspicion. It was hard to know what to believe or whom to trust. Even Captain Lasserre made her feel uncomfortable, though that clearly was paranoia.

Shelley wanted to be able to trust Jack Kincaid. His concern seemed genuine, although she recognized that he might have selfish motives in wanting her to stay with him. Ironically, that pleased her more than it frightened her. Their mutual attraction was no longer easy to deny.

This was no time to allow herself to become infatuated. Besides, her feelings were obviously a product of circumstances. Everyone knew that people had a tendency to let their guard down when they were away from home.

In Los Angeles, she would no more have gotten involved with Jack Kincaid than the man in the moon. True, she wasn't exactly involved with him now, but she'd certainly been thinking about it a lot. And, to be honest, she was tempted by the notion of a fling with him. She'd been testing the idea in her mind ever since the previous night.

But Shelley knew she wouldn't get anywhere by mulling it over and over in her mind. The best course of action for her right now was to concentrate on everything she had to do on Saint Maurice, and that meant getting the house in order.

She had Simone bring her some cartons from the cellar, then Shelley began emptying her uncle's clothes from his armoire and drawers. Most of the garments were old and probably not worth saving, but she would offer everything to the villagers before tossing them away.

After she'd disposed of the clothing, she rummaged through the mess the burglars had left. The contents of some old shoe boxes and the smaller drawers had been dumped onto the floor. Most of it was junk—odds and ends like coins, shoehorns, keys, pencils, cuff links, bow ties, cans of shoe polish, old postcards and other souvenirs.

However, buried in the pile was something unexpected—a fairly recent photograph of Chantal Favre in a bikini and a straw hat. And standing next to her, looking uncomfortable, was Henry Van Dam in his ubiquitous white suit and bow tie.

"Oh, my God," she murmured. "Chantal, you're a vixen."

SHELLEY AND SIMONE HAD lunch together at the kitchen table. Shelley had hoped to draw more gossip out of the woman, but Simone must have decided that she'd already said too much. When Shelley so much as mentioned Chantal and Henry in the same breath, Simone instantly fell mum. Apparently loyalties in the community weren't easy to break.

As they were cleaning up, they heard the Jeep, but it didn't stop. The sound of the engine faded and Shelley assumed it was Chantal driving the gendarmes back to the village.

After Simone returned to work, Shelley went outside to have a look at the garden. She had memories of strolling in it with her mother. Sadly, the beds were in sorry shape, the jungle having made its inroads. Feeling nostalgic, Shelley sat on an old stone bench at the top of the garden and looked out at the vista.

She searched for Jack's cottage, but was unable to see it. If she were down there with her swimsuit and an overnight bag, would he take it as a clear signal that she had a romantic interest in him? More importantly, perhaps, *did* she have an interest in him? And was that really what she wanted?

Shelley was daydreaming about Jack when she suddenly heard a noise in the brush. Assuming it was an animal, she quickly got to her feet. The rustling in the undergrowth continued and she saw something large looming toward her. She was on the verge of screaming when the foliage parted and Claude Perrin appeared.

He was not as wide-eyed as he'd been on the road that morning, but his face did register a great deal of apprehension. Shelley's heart was pounding heavily, but Claude looked as though his might be, as well. He'd stopped at the edge of the jungle, twenty feet from her, looking as though he was ready to plunge back into it if she made the slightest move.

She wiped the distressed look off her face and smiled. It brought no response. Claude was grimacing, though it was unlikely he intended any hostility. Shelley stood perfectly still, doing her best to appear friendly. After a moment or two, Claude began inching toward her.

He was dressed as he'd been the day before, in a coat that looked much too warm for the summer heat. After having traversed about half the distance to the place where she stood, Claude removed his hat, apparently as a sign of respect. His thin hair was damp with perspiration and plastered to his head.

As soon as he got close to her, he reached into his pocket and held up a photo for her to see. It was a picture of Claude with Henry. They were standing side by side, much as her uncle and Chantal had been in the photo she'd found earlier.

She nodded and smiled as though it pleased her to know they'd been friends.

Claude smiled back, then gestured for her to follow him, actually taking her by the arm. Shelley was apprehensive, but when he started leading her toward the house, she relaxed.

They arrived at the rear entrance to the laboratory. Shelley presumed that Claude probably wanted more plants, which she was more than willing to give him. But when she tried to go inside, he made a grunting sound and tried to pull her away.

"Don't you want another orchid?" she asked.

He obviously didn't understand, but she didn't know how else to tell him that she wanted to give him a present. She tried again to go in the door, but he was adamant. Claude pulled on her arm forcefully, leading her around the corner of the house. What was he doing? Claude was very strong. Could he want to hurt her?

They were stumbling past the side of the house when Simone came around the corner with a broom in her hand. She started running toward them, waving the broom threateningly, her skirts flying.

"*Monstre! Idiot!*" the woman shouted as she advanced on them.

Claude froze, making a strange rasping sound as he breathed. Shelley glanced at him and saw a terrified look on his face. All at once he released her arm and rushed back into the jungle.

Suddenly Simone came running up, short of breath. She put the broom down and leaned on it. "What a fool, that man! He never learns! Are you all right, *madame?* I am sorry for that."

Shelley was having a hard time recovering from the excitement herself. "Yes, I'm all right. Claude wasn't trying to hurt me. He was taking me someplace."

"Where? No, *madame*, he is crazy. And since his mother is no longer alive, he should be taken away. He passes more time in the jungle than in his house. No one knows what he is up to. For his own good, he should be taken away."

Shelley felt badly about what had happened. She didn't know Claude, but whatever he was up to, it didn't seem the product of madness to her. He had wanted to show her something. Yet what would he possibly have to show her?

If it was something in the house, why hadn't he gone inside with her? Could it have been something in front? Or was he trying to take her away from the house altogether?

"It's nothing to concern yourself about, Simone," Shelley said. "I don't think Claude has bad intentions."

"No, but he is crazy. That is certain. If you sleep in this house, you must have the doors and windows locked, *madame*. Who knows what is inside his head?"

Shelley realized that Simone was right. The wisest course would be to play it safe, which was still another reason to spend the night at Jack's place. Whatever dangers faced her there couldn't compare with the possibility of having to deal with a burglar, a murderer, or a poor disturbed soul.

They both went inside. Shelley headed upstairs to pack an overnight bag. She wasn't completely convinced that Claude was a danger, but Simone knew him a lot better than she did. And Jack would be the beneficiary of her uncertainty. She might be the beneficiary as well, she reflected, and smiled to herself.

She carried her case downstairs, leaving it in the entry hall. Simone was still scrubbing the walls in the salon, so Shelley thought it wise to remain until the other woman had finished for the day.

She entered the library, opened her purse and took out the photograph of her uncle and Chantal. She was very attractive, even alluring. And though Shelley found her a charming and engaging individual, she didn't quite trust her. Chantal was ambitious and determined, and she seemed to have only one thing on her mind.

After putting the photo back in her purse, she strode over to the window and peered out at the jungle that was only thirty yards from the house. Shelley picked out the approximate place where Claude had disappeared. Was the poor man still hiding there, waiting? Perhaps he was crouching in the foliage, watching the house, even spying on her at that very minute. Shelley shivered.

Sadly, she knew she was witnessing the gradual disintegration of her compassion for her fellow human beings. Fear was a terrible thing. It seemed that her weird, ridiculously eccentric uncle had, in death, dragged her into the most bizarre and frightening adventure of her life.

AN HOUR LATER, CHANTAL arrived with word that Philippe Dufour had called to say that he would be arriving on Saint Barts late the next morning. Chantal told him that Shelley would probably meet him at the airport.

"I hope that is okay," Chantal said. "I assumed you would be eager to talk with him."

"Yes, that's fine. Jack and I will be over there tomorrow anyway."

"I told Professeur Dufour that was likely so."

"Thank you, Chantal." Shelley tried to maintain the same friendly tone as before, but it was hard, considering the less-than-charitable thoughts she'd had about the woman since finding the picture. Of course, it was possible that their relationship had been entirely innocent, but Simone's slip about Chantal having an interest in Henry made it all the more likely there'd been intrigue of some sort.

Simone stepped into the entry hall where they were standing, and the two Frenchwomen started jabbering away. Shelley couldn't follow what was being said, except that Claude's name was mentioned.

"That explains why we can't find him," Chantal said to Shelley. "Captain Lasserre gathered the people in the vil-

lage for an interrogation, but no one could locate Claude."
She gave Shelley a sympathetic look. "I hope he didn't
frighten you too much."

"No, I'm sure it was innocent."

"He is probably harmless," Chantal told her, "but it
wouldn't hurt to be careful. My offer for you to stay at my
house is still good, if you wish to come."

Shelley glanced over at her overnight bag by the door,
realizing, to her surprise, that she wasn't feeling the least
bit of embarrassment about her decision to stay at Jack's.
"I'll probably sleep on Jack's sofa again. He's been a perfect gentleman, and anyway, I promised him a game of
chess. I'm determined to beat him."

"Jack is not one to beat easily," Chantal said, arching a
brow. "At anything. Anyway, you won't be using Henry's set. Captain Lasserre took it away."

"Oh?"

"Yes. The corners of the board are carved in a distinctive pattern. He said they matched the wound on Henry's
skull."

"Oh, my God. You mean my uncle was killed by someone hitting him over the head with a chessboard?"

"That is not certain, yet," Chantal replied. "But Lasserre
thinks it is likely."

"Good Lord."

"If you are concerned about Jack, don't be," Chantal
added, with her characteristic smile. "He is a lover, not a
killer." She turned for the door. "If you want a ride, Simone, I am going back to the village."

"*Bien,*" the cleaning woman responded. "I am ready."

A few minutes later Shelley was on the veranda, bid-
ding them goodbye. Chantal waved.

"*Au revoir, madame,*" Simone called out as they drove off.

As Shelley watched them disappear down the road, Chantal's comment about Jack reverberated in her head. "He is a lover, not a killer."

8

JACK KINCAID SAT ON HIS terrace, thinking about his confrontation with Guy Lasserre. "I think you should plan on staying close by Saint Maurice, *monsieur*," he'd said. "At least until the investigation is concluded."

"Are you saying, Captain, that you suspect me of killing Henry Van Dam?"

"I am saying the same thing to everyone on the island. I understand that the chessboard did not come into your possession until it was given to you by Madame Van Dam. However, you were a frequent visitor to *monsieur*'s house, you did play chess with him often, and you can't account for where you were the day he was murdered."

"I told you I was probably out sailing. It's been several weeks since Henry was killed, and unless I'm away flying, my days are pretty much indistinguishable."

"Please do not be in a hurry to defend yourself, Monsieur Kincaid. I am making no accusation. I am simply explaining why I want you to stay nearby."

"Tomorrow I'm supposed to fly Miss Van Dam to Saint Barts, and the day after that I have a charter out of Saint Martin. But I'll be back that evening. Does that qualify as staying nearby?"

"I see no problem in that."

"I'm not quite under house arrest, then."

"No, *monsieur*."

"I don't mean to tell you your business, Captain Lasserre, but out of curiosity, have you considered questioning Karl Baumann?"

"I have considered it, and I intend to speak to Monsieur Baumann. Any other questions?"

Jack had said no more. Instead he'd looked out at Chantal who'd been sitting in the Jeep, waiting. He'd long since learned how dangerous she could be. The woman was an opportunist of the highest order. It was good to keep her on his friendly side, though, and he had. He'd even made love with her a few times after he'd lost the heart for it. Chantal had sensed the change in his feelings and had promptly ended their sexual relationship a year or so ago.

Fortunately she, too, had elected to keep things friendly. The only issues he could honestly say they'd clashed over were the future of the island—and Henry. Not that they were separable—at least in Chantal's mind.

Jack had been edgy ever since Lasserre had arrived with the news of Henry's murder. Somebody was definitely playing hardball. It was hard to imagine that either Chantal or a big firm like Deitz-Langen would actually get involved in murder. Still, who besides the giant company had sufficient motivation?

The whole affair was confounding. Henry hadn't said or done anything to indicate that he believed his own life was in danger, other than his routine paranoid ramblings. Obviously there had been more to that than anybody realized.

Furthermore, he hadn't much liked it when Lasserre had carted off the suitcase filled with Henry's notebooks. He really had no reason to suspect that Lasserre was corrupt, but who could be sure? If Deitz-Langen was willing to offer Shelley a couple of million dollars for Henry's research, a few hundred thousand might well turn the head of a provincial police official living on a public servant's salary.

Come to think of it, he was puzzled about why Shelley had told the gendarmes about the notebooks in the first place, unless she'd gotten frightened, or didn't trust him anymore. Of course, she might be one of those people who were willing to put their lives in the hands of the police. Jack wasn't. Not because of any particular incident—it was his policy to trust his fellow man only after they'd proved themselves worthy of trust.

Jack hadn't had much opportunity to talk to Shelley since they'd been informed that Henry was murdered. Consequently he couldn't judge what she was thinking.

He had been hoping that she would show up for a swim. There had been something in her eyes when he'd extended the invitation—a look that told him she would come. But with women, nothing was ever certain.

It was possible, too, that Lasserre's posturing had made her change her mind and pull back. Shelley was a practical woman and probably not very big on sentimentality—she'd demonstrated her no-nonsense attitude from the beginning. The funny thing was, he wasn't quite sure what he would do if she did show up. It wouldn't be easy to go on playing the part of the good host indefinitely. At some point, his natural instincts would take over and something would happen.

What mystified him was why he was so concerned about what she thought, about whether she was coming or not. He wasn't afraid of rejection. Never had been. And yet, for some peculiar reason, he cared about Shelley Van Dam and what she thought.

Jack got up from his chair. The sun was hot, though the afternoon was wearing on. If Shelley wanted to go swimming, she'd have to show up soon.

He considered walking back up to the plantation house to see what was going on. The gendarmes would be interrogating the villagers, so Shelley would almost certainly be alone. Yet if she wanted to come, she would. He'd invited her. That was all he could do.

Tired of hanging around, he went inside, changed into his trunks and headed for the cove to go snorkeling. All his gear was on the boat. If Shelley did ever show up, she could find him there.

As he made his way down the path to the beach, he told himself he was devoting too much thought to Shelley Van Dam. After all, his interest in her was a passing thing. They were together only by chance and they were worlds apart—both figuratively and literally.

When he got down to his boat, Jack suddenly had the urge to go sailing that evening. He could make a loop of the island. That would be a good way to clear his head.

He waded out in the warm water until it came to just above his thighs. Standing there, he drew a breath of the balmy air and sighed. He loved his life, he really did. There weren't many men who could say that. He was one of the lucky ones.

Then he turned and looked up to the path at the top of the cliff, hoping to see Shelley, but she wasn't there. A twinge of disappointment shot through him.

God, he wasn't falling for her, was he?

JACK CLIMBED THE LADDER on the side of the boat, tossed his snorkel, mask and fins onto the deck, then wearily sat on the gunwale. He'd been in the water an hour and had gotten some good exercise. The exhaustion felt good.

Looking up, he detected a flicker of motion. Then a familiar cap of blond curls came into view, followed by her bare shoulders . . . her bare . . . waist and hips. God, was Shelley naked? No, she had on a suit. A damned skimpy one. A string bikini.

Shelley stopped and faced the boat, raising her hand to shield her eyes from the sun. Then she spotted him and waved.

"Ahoy!" she called. "Am I too late?"

"No," he called back to her. "Come on out."

"I changed in your house and left my things there. I hope that's okay."

"Of course. What's mine is yours."

"What?"

"Come on down," he said.

Jack was amazed. He hadn't quite expected anything this overt. Of course, she might turn out to be a tease. Some women got off on that.

Jack kept his eyes on her as she walked toward the boat. Shelley had a dynamite figure. She had full, shapely breasts. Her waist was tiny, her hips nicely rounded, and she had terrific legs.

Her feet were in the water and she was slowly moving toward him, her eyes fixed on him, just as his were on her. Her bikini was bright red. Damn, if his heart wasn't racing.

"Water's perfect," she called as the sea reached her thighs.

"Not as perfect as you, honey," he mumbled to himself.

She plunged in and started swimming. Her strokes were even and smooth, if not powerful. Jack watched her approach, knowing he'd been stung. Why did men have to have this weakness? It was going to be hell, keeping his hands off her.

Shelley arrived at the base of the ladder. With her hair wet and slicked back, her delicate bone structure was more evident. He'd recalled she was attractive, but now she looked positively beautiful.

She was treading water, gazing up at him. Jack gave her one of his mischievous looks.

"Do you know the password?"

"Yeah," she replied. "Let me aboard or I'll scuttle your boat."

"That'll do. Come on up."

Shelley grabbed the ladder. As soon as she reached the top, he took her hand, helping her on board.

"What an unexpected pleasure," Jack said, handing her a towel.

Shelley took it and wiped her face. "Unexpected? You invited me to go snorkeling, didn't you?"

"I was referring to the suit."

"Gentlemen don't make remarks like that, Jack."

"Yesterday was my day this week to be a gentleman."

"So what are you now?"

"Whatever the opposite is."

She threw the towel at him and went over to the roof of the deckhouse, where she sat down. "I suggest you borrow your day to be a gentleman from next week."

"You know, I've always wondered why women dress to make men weak, then criticize them for their weakness."

"I don't know about other women, but I dress like this to go swimming."

"My compliments on the unintended effect."

Shelley folded her arms defiantly. "I thought I'd be safe wearing a bikini in the French West Indies. The norm here is to swim and sunbathe topless, isn't it?"

"Yep. So maybe it's you, not your suit." He sat on the gunwale across from her, his arms folded like hers.

She observed him for a moment or two. "Tell me straight, Jack, did I make a mistake in coming here?"

"Define *mistake*."

She grinned. "You know what I mean."

"Forgive me if I'm gushing—it's an honest reaction—but you're a hell of an attractive lady."

"It's unfortunate it takes a bikini for you to notice."

"Define *unfortunate*," he said.

She leaned over and grabbed the towel lying on the deck and tossed it at him again. "You've got a mouth, Kincaid."

He shrugged, having fun teasing her.

"Are we going snorkeling?" she asked. "Or are we just going to sit here and ogle?"

"I'll sacrifice. Let's go snorkeling." He got up and went to the stairs leading down into the cabin. "I'll get your gear."

Without a doubt it was going to be a painful evening if he didn't at least find out how she really felt about him.

THE ENTIRE TIME THEY were in the water Shelley felt like a minnow swimming with a shark. Jack never touched her, but she could sense his proximity. At times she almost felt enveloped by him. The bikini was probably a mistake—if that's what caused it.

The cove was a wonderful place to snorkel. The water was clear and the variety of fish remarkable. Shelley had snorkeled a fair amount in Hawaii and Tahiti, though she hardly considered herself an expert. A couple of times they dove together and swam for fifteen yards or so along the bottom, side by side, schools of brightly colored fish parting before them. When an old sea turtle wandered into the cove, they chased him until he became annoyed and went back out to sea.

They finally climbed aboard the boat and stretched out on a pair of deck mats to dry off. The sun was getting low, but it was still quite warm. Shelley lay on her stomach and looked over at Jack, who was on his back and staring up at the sky, his brows and mustache and lashes glistening.

"You do have an idyllic life," she said.

He turned toward her. "Idyllic? I thought you'd decided I led a selfish life."

"Well, you do. But I'm beginning to understand why you're so happy here."

"Funny. Earlier I was wondering if I'm really as happy as I thought I was."

"Why's that?"

"Some woman came along and told me I ought to be battling the ills of humanity instead of pampering myself. Funny how that can turn a man's feelings of contentment into guilt."

"If you're trying to blame me for any pangs of conscience you're having, you can forget it, Jack. You and your island are corrupting me as much as I'm corrupting you."

"How so?"

"I find myself slowing down, and I'm starting to smell the flowers a little, as they say. When I think of the way I acted at the airport in Saint Thomas, I get embarrassed."

"Now, that is a quick conversion," he said, rolling onto his side. He supported his head with his hand and smiled at her.

"It's not a conversion, it's an awareness."

"That's a start, anyway, kiddo."

Shelley propped herself up on her elbow, facing Jack. They looked into each other's eyes as the sea lapped at the hull of the boat. The only other sounds were the waves against the rocks out beyond the mouth of the cove and the occasional call of a seabird.

After several moments he reached over and touched her face. Neither of them broke eye contact. Shelley felt the sexual awareness between them. It had been inevitable, and she had set it in motion by coming to him. Yet she knew she hadn't consciously intended that things would work out this way. It had been more a matter of letting things evolve naturally.

In ways she was being seduced by both Saint Maurice and Jack Kincaid. The terrible business about her uncle was hovering over them, though. Shelley wanted to escape all that for a bit. She wanted the safety and comfort of Jack Kincaid's arms. It was no more complicated than that, but it wasn't until now—at this moment—that she fully acknowledged it.

Jack edged closer, his face moving toward hers easily and naturally. When his lips brushed against hers, she began to fill with the sensation of him, his taste, his feel.

At first the kiss remained tender, an overture, their initial connection. The longer his mouth lingered, the more demanding it became. He eased still closer, his chest coming up against her moist skin.

Shelley rolled onto her back and Jack moved over her, his hand grasping the small of her waist, his tongue sinking between her parting lips. He slipped his fingers under the edge of her top and pulled it up, exposing her breast.

He touched her nipple, rolling the bud between his thumb and finger as he continued kissing her. Her nipple hardened and began to tingle. Within seconds, her entire body came alive.

When Jack started licking her breasts, Shelley shut her eyes and felt a rush of warm liquid between her legs. Never had she been aroused so quickly, or so thoroughly. But when Jack's hand moved to the edge of her bikini bottom, she knew she had to get control of herself. She grabbed his wrist, stopping him.

Jack lifted his head and looked into her eyes. Shelley blinked with sudden embarrassment and glanced away, still holding his wrist just below her navel.

"Whew!" she said, trying to calm her pounding heart. "You really ought to get a patent on that. Bottle it and you won't ever have to work again."

She took a peek at him to check his reaction and was relieved to see a smile. "You inspire me."

"Yeah, but I think you've had some practice." She pushed his hand aside and pulled the top of her bikini back over her breast.

Jack kissed her lips again and she had to fight herself to keep from kissing him back. "You didn't like it?"

She sighed. "A little too much."

"How can you like something too much?"

"I'd intended to stay in the cottage with you tonight, Jack. How can I, if this sort of thing is going on?"

He ran his finger along the edge of her top. "It seems to me this sort of thing and staying with someone goes together."

"It's clearly what *you* have in mind, but—"

"But you didn't?"

"I didn't intend for things to go quite this fast."

"How fast did you intend things to go?"

She whacked him on the arm. "Don't ask so many questions."

He leaned over and pressed his lips against hers—tenderly, so that she could feel the softness. Shelley couldn't resist the affection. She ran her fingers through his hair, then trailed them down his neck and across his shoulder, thinking it would be so easy to have an affair with him.

He took her hand and kissed it. "Is this better?" he murmured.

"Oh, yes, a slow death is so much better than a quick one."

"I'm not sure I follow the logic."

"I'm not sure I do, either. Maybe I just need to feel comfortable with what's happening."

Jack caressed her shoulder in an affectionate, loving way. "I'm sorry if I rushed you."

She looked into his eyes, feeling tugged in two directions. A part of her wanted to embrace him, to make love with him. The other part was trying to be reasonable. She ran her finger along the edge of his mustache. "I don't know if I've ever kissed a man with a mustache before."

"Did it tickle?"

"Sort of. It was different." She smiled. "I liked it."

He gave her another kiss. "Good."

Her expression turned serious. "I'm not playing with you, Jack. I mean, I'm not trying to be a tease, in case you're thinking that. It's just that I'm having trouble throwing caution to the winds."

"What are you afraid of? Enjoying it too much?"

She was inclined to say no. How could she be afraid of enjoying herself too much? Then she thought it over and admitted the idea made some sense.

It wasn't as if having sex was some kind of monumental event. She wasn't a virgin. And neither was she committed to Warren. She was single and free to do what she wanted. So why did she hesitate? Jack Kincaid turned her on. Maybe she *was* afraid of enjoying it too much. She scooted away and sat up, adjusting the top of her suit.

"Maybe being afraid is the best proof that making love with you is not a very good idea," she said.

"Nothing worthwhile would ever get done, if people let their fears govern them."

"Considering the circumstances, Jack, that's a very self-serving statement."

He laughed and sat up, too. "I plan on taking you sailing this evening. Question is if we go before or after dinner."

"You're giving me a choice?"

"Sure, why not? Depends if you like sunsets or moonlit nights better."

She pondered her decision.

"Tell you what," he said, "we can watch the sunset and stay out until the moon comes up. How does that sound?"

"Have it all, you mean?"

"Yeah."

"What about dinner?"

Jack smiled. "Some things are better when you have to wait for them."

THE SUN WAS JUST BARELY above the horizon by the time they left the cove under the power of the auxiliaries. The wind was indifferent and Jack wasn't sure they'd be going very far until it picked up.

He asked Shelley to do something now and then, but mostly she lay back and watched him maneuver the ketch. He was still in his swim trunks, though he'd slipped on a pair of deck shoes so that he wouldn't lose his footing. When he settled down beside her and took the wheel, his deeply tanned shoulders and arms were gleaming with a light sheen of perspiration.

Apart from looking at her in a way that said making love was on his mind, Jack did nothing overt. He didn't touch her except in the most casual way. He didn't kiss her. He treated her more like her long-term lover than an incipient one. And somehow, that made Shelley want him all the more.

"Do you live this way so you can avoid dealing with all the unpleasant stuff out in the world?" she asked, as the boat drifted along under nearly slack sails.

Jack squinted at the setting sun. "That's a big part of it, I guess."

"Over the past few hours I've learned to understand it better," she said.

"Don't tell me you're about to become a convert."

"No, but now I'm able to appreciate the temptation." She looked over the gunwale at Saint Maurice, lying half a mile or so away, its dense jungle and rocky shore faintly visible in the twilight. "By all rights I should be feeling anxious and upset, considering what we found out about Uncle Henry today. But I'm at peace. What do you think is going to happen next? Is Captain Lasserre competent, or is he going to bungle the investigation?"

"I don't really know the man, but I wouldn't expect great feats of criminal detection from him. As for the killer, about all I can tell you is that it isn't me."

"I know you couldn't have done it, Jack," she said with conviction. "I can believe you guilty of a lot of things, but not that."

"I suppose that's a vote of confidence," he responded wryly. "Frankly, I wasn't sure what you'd think."

"The truth is, I don't want to think about it at all, right now." She ran her fingers back through her hair and stretched her arms. "I'm glad I came sailing with you. I feel safe and content here. The thought of being alone in the plantation house sends shivers down my spine."

"Because of a murderer running loose?"

"That and maybe because I'm a coward. I had another scare this afternoon, though it turned out to be nothing."

"What happened?"

She told him about Claude Perrin's bizarre visit, and the way he'd tried to drag her around the house. "What do you suppose he was trying to do?"

"I have no idea, Shelley. Claude's odd."

"He's not crazy, Jack. He's handicapped. He was trying to communicate the only way he knew how. I just don't know what he was trying to say."

He smiled at her, the last glow of the sunset illuminating his face, warming the tones of his skin. "You're good-hearted. I like that. It's a nice trait."

"You say it as though it's coming as a complete surprise," she said.

"I pretty well had you figured as a single-minded dynamo, who ran over things when it was easier than running around them."

"Was I really that bad?"

"It was probably my own sensitivities as much as it was you," he said.

"I figured you were a self-centered, thoroughly dissipated playboy," she admitted.

"God, and I thought I was pretty cute."

"I noticed that about you, too," she said with a laugh.

Jack reached over and cuffed her gently. Shelley touched his hand. He moved close enough to give her a long, emotional kiss that did a lot more than just set her on fire. When their lips parted she felt something for him that was deep and strong. It was more devastating than simple lust, yet she knew that was part of it, too.

Jack lightly stroked her jaw with his knuckles. "If you're hungry or thirsty, I can probably find a few crackers and some soft drinks or something below," he said, his voice practically a whisper.

She was hungry, all right, but how could she admit that it was for him? "Maybe something to drink," she said.

The boat was hardly moving, so Jack simply abandoned the wheel and went below. Shelley looked up at the darkening sky and sighed. The man was either a magician or she was falling for him.

It was incredible if she stopped to think about it. Could it mean something, or was she simply needy and living out a fantasy? Never before had she considered making love for the physical pleasure alone, yet there was something about Jack Kincaid that made her consider all sorts of things that she had never dared to dream about with other men.

He came back a few minutes later. His arms were full. "One stale box of crackers," he said, beginning the inventory, "a can of sardines, two cans of cola and a quarter of a bottle of rum. Does that sound like a feast, or what?"

He handed her two empty coffee mugs and eased down beside her. Looking up at the sky, he said, "If a wind doesn't come up soon, we may be stranded here for a week. Can you live that long on rum?"

"Better than on sardines, I can promise you that."

Jack opened a can of cola. "Hope you don't mind this stuff warm."

"Everything is relative, isn't it?"

He poured some cola into both mugs, then opened the rum. "Care for some?"

Shelley did. "All right."

He poured two or three splashes of rum into each mug as she held them. Then he opened the box of crackers and set it between them. Taking his drink, he clinked it against hers, took a sip, and lay back, putting an arm behind his head.

Shelley sipped her drink and watched him, marveling. What was she feeling just then? Was it infatuation? Self-delusion? Loneliness? Or was Jack Kincaid somebody special?

He inhaled. "Ever known anything like this before?"

She looked down at his chest, wanting to put her hands on it, to kiss it. She took a big slug of the rum and cola—so big it made her eyes water. Then she shook her head. "No. No, I haven't."

He casually took her hand and began toying with her fingers. "Funny thing is, I haven't either. Not quite like this."

She didn't believe him, but it didn't matter; she was glad he'd said it. She drank some more, looking at him over the rim of her mug, sure now that she did want to make love with him. Should she touch him first, or wait for him to touch her?

When she'd finished her drink, Jack gave her only a little more, perhaps knowing he shouldn't let her have too much. She lay back, nursing the second drink. Her head was already light and she felt a pleasant buzz.

The sky was virtually black, and the breeze had fallen to a dead calm. Jack offered her a cracker, but she wasn't hungry. He quietly munched on one, occasionally sipping his drink.

Finally she couldn't stand the mounting tension any longer. She reached over and put her hand on his. "When are you going to make love to me?" she whispered.

He didn't look surprised, though she could tell by the slight smile that touched his lips that he was pleased. "As soon as the moon comes up."

"When will that be?"

He looked at Saint Maurice, silhouetted against the night sky. "Less than half an hour from now."

"Why do we have to wait?"

"Because first we're going to take off our suits and go for a swim in the sea."

9

HE WATCHED AS SHE untied the top of her suit and let it fall away. She was so luscious, so inviting. But he didn't move. Only his eyes shifted back and forth between her face and breasts.

She got to her feet and went to the side of the boat. Steadying herself, she untied the bottom of her suit and let it drop to the deck. It was completely dark now, but the ambient light of the night sky enabled him to see her silhouette. He swallowed hard. She was so lovely.

"Aren't you coming, Jack? Or was this a trick to get me naked?"

He got up and slowly inched his suit down over his hips. She stared at his phallus, her gaze becoming more and more intense until the awareness of what was happening unnerved her and she looked away.

Jack wanted her. He'd had enough of the game and started moving toward her. But, seeing his intention, Shelley turned and dove over the side of the boat, disappearing under the surface of the water.

He leaned over the gunwale but couldn't spot her anywhere. When ten seconds had passed and she didn't appear, he began to worry. Had she blacked out? He was about to dive in when she surfaced fifteen yards or so from the ketch.

"It's fabulous!" she called out, exhilarated. "It's like a bathtub! I think I'll swim to Saint Martin." She turned then and began swimming away, into the night.

Jack didn't know if she'd had too much to drink or was just teasing him, but he wasn't going to take any chances. He dove in after her, feeling his adrenaline pumping. She must have seen him coming because she started stroking at a furious pace. It took him nearly a minute to catch her. He grabbed her by the foot.

Shelley stopped swimming as soon as he touched her, giggling like a teenager.

"Hey, where do you think you're going?" he said between breaths.

"I have to put up a fight, don't I? Isn't that what men expect?"

Her face was so lively and beautiful that it hurt just to look at her. They were treading water, facing each other. The sea was calm. Shelley inched toward him. When she was close enough, she reached out, took his face in her hands and kissed him hard on the mouth. She writhed against him, her breasts sliding back and forth over his chest.

They sank beneath the surface, and when they came up they were both gasping for air. Shelley laughed joyfully. She rubbed his chest with her hand, taunting him. Jack couldn't stand the slow pace, so he took hold of her waist, pulling her hard against him, kissing her.

With his arms around her, they couldn't stay afloat, so she moved away a bit, treading water. He reached out and caressed her breast until the nipple got hard. She responded by running her hand down between his legs, taking him in her hand and stroking him. He soon grew so hard that the throbbing hurt. He felt as though he might burst. He had to have her.

"Have you ever made love in the sea?" he murmured, reaching for her.

She released him then and moved away. "Sounds like a good way to drown."

"What a way to go."

This was the damnedest seduction he'd ever experienced. No woman had ever turned him on this way. He really wanted her, but he held back, watching her.

"God, Jack," she said, her voice filled with wonder. "Look at that sky, and the stars. This is absolutely marvelous. I've never seen the world from this perspective or felt anything like this before."

At one level he could appreciate what she was saying, but it was difficult to focus on anything but having her. "It's a first for me, too."

"If I were to drown right now," she went on, "if this were to be my last minute on earth, it would be all right."

"No, it wouldn't."

"Why not?"

"Because you haven't paid me yet."

She splashed him and retorted, "Don't talk like that. You'll ruin everything."

He looked around for the ketch and was startled when he couldn't locate it in the darkness. "I hate to be the bearer of sad tidings, but we may have lost our boat."

She jerked herself upright. "What?" She stared into the murky night along with him. "Oh, God."

"It's over there somewhere. Come on."

They started swimming and the ketch soon came into view. She stopped and grinned happily. "Thank goodness!" She gave him a kiss.

"You know, my dear," he said, "you don't seem at all like the woman I picked up in Saint Thomas."

"I don't think I am."

"To what do we owe this change?"

"Maybe it's the climate." She laughed as she took smooth efficient strokes toward the boat. By the time they got there, she was tired and breathing heavily. She took hold of the ladder. "You have to be a gentleman and turn around."

"Suddenly I have to be a gentleman?"

"Suddenly I'm sober," she replied.

He brushed his body against hers. "We'll have to do something about that, won't we?"

"No," she replied. "If I drink any more, I may jump over the side again, and I might not make it back a second time."

"Perhaps I should tie you down," he said, taking hold of her.

She writhed free and made him turn his back. "I'm getting out now." She climbed the ladder and after a minute said, "You can come aboard."

He found her standing on the deck with a towel wrapped around her. She tossed a towel at him and turned and walked along the deck. Jack dried himself, then secured the towel around his waist.

She was at the bow, looking out to sea, when he came up behind her and kissed the nape of her neck. She turned, seeming terribly small. She touched his face.

"I want you, Shelley," he said.

Her eyes turned glossy, but she didn't say anything. Instead she ran her finger across his nipple. "Would you hold me for a minute first?" she asked.

He took her into his arms, and when he looked out over the water he saw the moon rising behind Saint Maurice. Shelley turned to look also.

"It's beautiful," she said.

For a few moments they stared at it, content in each other's arms. Then he took her face in his hands, peering into her eyes, questioning.

"Thanks for not rushing me. I'm a little nervous," she said.

"Maybe I am, too." It was nerves, in a way, and frustration at the slow pace. He was eager to find out how it would be with her, and holding back was difficult. Her flesh felt so good. She was so lovely.

When she lifted her mouth and kissed him, there was no holding back. He unfastened her towel and it fell to the deck. Then he scooped her into his arms and carried her to where the deck pads were spread out. He knelt, laying her down. Then he got to his feet and backed off a few steps so that he could see her entire body naked in the moonlight.

SHELLEY LAY THERE before him, one arm behind her head, knowing he was coveting her. His face seemed almost solemn. Strangely, the distance he was keeping, his stillness, made the moment even more erotic. Then, when he removed the towel from his waist, she looked at him and quivered.

He knelt beside her. He was so close and yet he hadn't touched her. Finally he put his hand on her stomach.

She felt her heart pounding.

Then he leaned over and kissed one breast, swirling his tongue around the nipple a few times before sucking it gently. Shelley moaned. Her eyes closed and she lost herself in sensation. This was what she wanted.

After a few minutes he slid his hand between her legs, making her tense momentarily. But his touch was gentle and she began to relax. He stroked her softly, raising her excitement. She began throbbing where he touched her and soon the sensation spread through her whole body. There was a rush of warm liquid, then Jack's finger slid inside her. He drew it firmly against her nub, making her tremble.

She lay moaning with each stroke, his finger gliding in and out of her, making her ache for him. Her legs opened wider. She couldn't wait any longer. "Take me, Jack," she begged. "Please take me."

He moved on top of her and she wrapped her legs around his hips. She felt him place the tip of his erection against her opening. Then, when he cocked his hips, she felt him glide inside, filling her.

"Oh, God," he groaned from deep within his throat. "You feel wonderful."

Shelley dug her fingers into his back, pulling him against her, but Jack lay motionless, obviously trying to get control of himself. She squeezed him inside and he slowly began to thrust, drawing halfway out of her before sinking in again. The motion was repeated again and again, the rhythm quickening as he first withdrew, then surged into her.

The pulsing in her built with each thrust. She surrendered herself to the pleasure, the needs of her body dictating her movements. Jack was heaving against her so forcefully that she was soon on the brink of orgasm.

Then it came, rising from deep within her, wave after wave rippling through her. She cried out at the pleasure, her voice piercing the night air. Their bodies heaved together a final time, then they collapsed in exhaustion.

Shelley's heart was pounding so hard she couldn't get enough air into her lungs. Jack had to lift himself away from her so that she could breathe. Sweat was pouring from his brow and her face was wet, as well. Her breasts and his chest were soaked.

"Oh, Lord," she mumbled as she drew her hands down the sides of his face. "I think I just died."

Jack was breathing deeply. "If so, then this is heaven."

"Is it ever." She lowered her legs to the pad, completely drained. Her arms dropped to her side, though Jack was still inside her.

The frenzy became an intensely warm glow. She was content, liking the feel of him inside her. He kissed her swollen lips and she looked into his eyes, feeling a far deeper emotion than she had before. He smiled, his face illuminated by the moon.

"You're rather proficient at this, aren't you?" she asked.

"You're no slouch," he told her.

"I don't want to bolster your ego unduly," Shelley said with a sigh, "but it has never been like that for me before." As she spoke, she was aware of the waning pulses deep within her. "I'm still coming, as a matter of fact."

"You've got a special talent," he said modestly. "It's obviously you."

"Don't all your women tell you you're fabulous?"

"You're the only woman I care to think about right now, okay?"

"Jack," she murmured, wedging her hands between them, "I think you'd better get off of me now. You're heavy."

He rolled away, leaving her feeling empty. He sighed with contentment. Had he gotten what he wanted? Of course, there wasn't really anything wrong with that. Hadn't it been just pleasure for her, too?

Jack groped for her hand as he stared up at the blanket of stars. He pulled her fingers to his lips. "You said earlier that you hadn't seen the world like this before. I kind of have that feeling myself. I've been out here a thousand times, but it hasn't looked like this."

"You don't need to make speeches to make me feel good," she said. "I can keep what happened in perspective."

He rolled his head toward her, trying to understand. He touched her cheek. "Are you upset?"

She lifted herself up on her elbow. "No, I've had my pleasure and now it's over. I feel good. You gave me a hell of an orgasm, so why would I be upset?"

Jack rose up on his elbow, too. "That doesn't ring true, if you don't mind me saying so."

"What do you expect, professions of love?"

He took her chin in his hand. "Listen, you little twit, we shared something very beautiful and special. I'd appreciate it if you wouldn't be so disparaging."

There was a touch of anger in his voice, and most definitely disapproval. She was surprised. "I told you I enjoyed it," she protested.

Jack pulled her to him and kissed her firmly on the mouth. It was a possessive kiss. When it was over he said, "I'm not a trained seal. I didn't make love just for the sex, or to please you. And I don't think *you* were in it just for fun, either."

He got up then, and without a word dove into the dark water. For a moment she lay in a daze. What the hell had happened? What was he suggesting?

A couple of minutes later he climbed up the ladder at the other end of the boat, his body glistening in the moonlight. But she was too distracted to consider what a wonderful specimen he was. Her mind was still on his last words—perhaps even more on his tone—what was implied but not spoken.

He went into the cabin and she covered herself with his towel. She lay there, staring at the speckled ribbon of stars overhead. She was beginning to understand what she'd been afraid to think only a few minutes ago: Jack Kincaid had come to mean more to her than she was willing to admit; Jack Kincaid was very special.

SHELLEY STEPPED OUT OF the shower into the tiny candle-lit bathroom of Jack's cottage. Looking into the small wood-framed mirror over the basin, she ran her comb through her tangled hair and stared at herself. She was still glowing, though it had been hours since they'd made love. And something else was different about her, too. She was no longer the same person. This night had changed a lot of things.

Jack had been sweet to her after he'd returned from changing his clothes. He'd brought her a dry towel and an old sweatshirt from the cabin. Then, while they waited for a breeze to come up, they'd snuggled together, talking about all kinds of things—their favorite foods, their marriages, their childhoods. Jack had a half brother in Ohio he hadn't seen in ten years, and that was the only family either of them had.

"You know," she'd told him as she lay in the protective curve of his arm, "we've had hardly any common experiences, except for having both lost our parents and having read some of the same books."

"I visited Disneyland the time my dad took me to California, right after my mother died," he said. "So I've been to L.A. once."

"Yes, and I came here once with my parents. Other than that, our worlds have been totally separate. You don't know mine and I don't know yours."

"You know mine now," he'd corrected.

"Yes," she'd admitted. "That much has changed."

When a breeze had finally come up, it was feeble, but sufficient to get them back to the cove. After Jack had an-

chored the ketch, they'd swum ashore and then climbed
the path to the cottage. By that time it was nearly mid-
night.

They'd nibbled on crackers while on the boat, but Jack
had insisted they had to eat a proper meal before they went
to bed. So, while she got cleaned up, he'd started dinner.

Crossing the sitting room, a candle in hand, Shelley
found Jack at the stove, stirring some packaged onion
soup. He glanced at her. The corner of his mustache
twitched as he nodded his approval over the black sundress she'd put on. "How lovely."

She smiled and set her candle down, going to him when
he beckoned to her. Still stirring the soup, Jack tucked her
under his arm, and she gave him a big hug. "I look like a
drowned rat and you know it," she said.

"You're one rat I'll let on my boat anytime." He kissed
her forehead.

Shelley peered into the pan. "Hmm, that smells good."

"Straight from the package."

There was another, larger pan, steaming on the back
burner. "What's that?"

"Tortellini out of the box. I don't live as barbarically as
you think," he replied. "I only look like Robinson Crusoe."

In minutes everything was ready. They agreed to eat on
the veranda. Shelley carried out the food while Jack un-
corked a bottle of *vin de table*, pouring some into tum-
blers.

"To the sweetest little rat I know," he said, toasting her.

Shelley self-consciously ran her fingers through her
damp hair. "A compliment I'll carry with me the rest of my
life."

She ate her soup with relish, now fully appreciating how
hungry she was. She started wolfing down the pasta when

she glanced up and saw Jack watching her, his chin resting on his folded hands.

"You aren't eating," she said.

"I'm savoring the sight of you. It's one I hope to carry with me the rest of my life."

"Is that romantic talk intentional or unintentional?" she asked, fingering her glass.

"Intentional."

"Why do you say it?"

"I've enjoyed this evening as much as any in my life, Shelley. I'll remember it always."

She sipped her wine, studying him over the glass. "Don't make too much of it."

"Why not? I have to tell you, this is the first time in a long time I've preferred being with somebody to being alone."

She set down her glass. "That's a nice thing to say."

"I'm not being nice. I mean it."

"Maybe I'm a little different from the company you're used to," she said.

"A lot different."

"It's the novelty, then."

He picked up his glass and took a sip of wine. "You seem to want to discourage me."

"From what?"

"From liking you. Too much, I mean."

"Do you like me?"

He leaned back, grinning. "Whatever my gut tells me is what I feel. And right now I feel pretty good about you. I feel real good about having you around."

"You know it's temporary, Jack. Anyway, I had you pegged for the love-'em-and-leave-'em type. You don't strike me as a guy who . . . gets sentimental."

He chuckled. "I get sentimental, as you call it. I just don't feel an obligation to get sentimental simply because I'm with someone. With you, I happen to feel a little different, and I'm telling you so."

"Thank you."

What was he trying to tell her? That he loved her? Or that he was on the verge of loving her?

The question made her uncomfortable, because she'd been struggling to put the evening into perspective herself. She'd been trying to tell herself that all that had happened was that she'd had sex. Period. But something was nagging at her, making her uneasy. The fact was, she liked Jack Kincaid. She liked him too damned much.

When he didn't say anything, she said, "Maybe we ought to change the subject."

"What would you prefer to talk about? Los Angeles? Your job?"

"I love my job and I love my home, but I don't want to talk about them."

"What about the guy you've been seeing . . . what's-his-name. Do you want to talk about him?"

"His name is Warren, and no, I don't want to talk about him, either."

Jack pushed his half-eaten plate of food away and rocked back in his chair. "You don't like the fact that it was so good between us, isn't that it? Not being in the habit of sleeping around for pleasure, you don't feel right about what happened."

"That's an approximation," she admitted, "but probably close enough to being true."

"What are we going to do about it?"

"There's nothing to do. It happened. That's all."

"So now we should forget about it?"

"Earthshaking sex is no reason to get serious over someone," she shot back. "I think we've got to put it behind us."

"And pretend it didn't happen?"

She didn't like his persistence on the issue. "Well, yes. Why not?"

Jack stared at her for a long time. "Things are getting so hostile, apparently we like each other a little too much," he said, getting to his feet. "If you'll excuse me, I'm going to grab a quick shower and get the salt off me. Just leave the dishes," he added, starting for the door. "I'll do them later."

"Jack..."

He stopped and looked back at her, the light from the lantern casting deep shadows across his face.

"I'm sorry I was testy. I'm not used to feeling like this."

"I understand," he replied. "I'm not, either."

He went inside and Shelley sighed. How terrible it was to get involved with someone you had no business being with. Some women might have been able to have a fling and forget about it, but she couldn't. That simply wasn't her nature.

She started to sip her wine when she remembered that it was the drinking that had gotten her into trouble earlier—or at least, she decided, it was convenient to blame it on the rum. She put down the glass and strolled to the edge of the terrace.

It was a lovely night. She inhaled the marvelous sea air, her mind conjuring up the image of their nude bodies on the deck. Their lovemaking had been so primal, so elemental. Maybe it was the naturalness of it all, the lack of complication, which had freed her to enjoy it so. Of course, Jack was a critical factor. She wouldn't have enjoyed it the same way with Warren. God, she thought, smiling at the irony, what had she gotten herself into?

She started walking out to the point. It wasn't more than fifty feet from the edge of the terrace, but it was beyond the ring of light cast by the lantern.

Standing there, she could see the scattered lights of vessels far out at sea. In the distant darkness she could see Saint Martin, a dim glow of light. This really was a different world. What would it be like to live here, as Jack did?

The night was strangely quiet. Even the waves, lapping at the rocks below, hardly made a sound. And yet, Shelley heard something, or more likely sensed something. Another presence.

Turning, she was startled by the figure of a man standing some fifteen feet away. With the lantern behind him, she could see only his silhouette. He was short and stocky, his clothes were baggy and he was wearing a hat. Though she was unable to see his face, Shelley knew instantly that it was Claude Perrin.

He took a step toward her, his hand extended. She backed up half a step, but knew she couldn't go any farther. The cliff was right behind her. It was only thirty or forty feet down and the drop wasn't completely vertical, but trying to escape that way, she could break her neck.

Claude took another step toward her. She didn't know what he intended, but he scared her. Knowing she was trapped, she was terrified.

"Jack!" she shouted. "Jack!"

Claude took another step and she screamed in desperation. Jack suddenly appeared on the terrace. He was in his shorts, apparently having run out directly from the bathroom.

"Claude!" he shouted. "What the hell are you doing?"

Claude didn't so much as flinch. Shelley realized why. The poor man was deaf. She pointed over his shoulder, trying to get him to turn around. Jack started picking his way across the rocks in his bare feet.

Claude turned then and, seeing Jack, let out a weird shriek of his own. Panicking, he started to run. Jack tried to grab him, but Claude shoved him away, sending him sprawling.

Shelley had been petrified, but Jack was such a comical sight, sprawled out on the ground in his underwear, that she began to laugh. He got up and hobbled over to her. "What the hell was that all about?" he demanded, clearly annoyed.

Shelley shook her head, still laughing. "I don't know. I just walked out here to enjoy the air and suddenly Claude popped up out of nowhere."

"Apparently I'm not your only admirer," Jack said, the corner of his mouth twitching. He reached for her hand, pulling her away from the edge of the cliff. "Come on inside. I see I'm going to have to keep a closer eye on you."

When they got to the terrace, he picked up the lantern and led her back inside. He put the lamp on the table, then gave her a stern look.

"You've certainly brought some excitement into my life. As if burglary and murder aren't enough, now you've got old Claude after you. Life around you certainly isn't boring, my dear."

She shivered, the humor in the situation having fled as quickly as it came. "Personally, I could do with a little boredom."

Jack must have sensed her change of mood, because he pulled her against him. She put her arms around him, feeling secure for the first time since Claude had reappeared.

Jack kissed her hair. "There's good news and bad news," he said. "The bad news is I can't lock this place up. Claude or anybody else could come right into the living room if he wanted to badly enough. The good news is there's plenty of room in my bed for you. It seems you've got a choice between Claude and me."

Shelley was in no mood to resist. "I guess I'll take the lesser of the two evils." Taking his arm, she went with him to the bedroom, rationalizing that there were a heck of a lot worse ways to feel safe than sleeping in Jack Kincaid's arms.

10

SHELLEY AWOKE TO THE sensation of the warm sun on her face. She was naked, and in Jack's bed. She sighed with contentment. Recollections of the night before came tumbling through her mind.

How many more times had they made love? It was at least three altogether, maybe four. They'd made love half the night, with little stretches of sleep in between. Once they'd climbed into bed they'd been unable to keep their hands off each other. She was as bad as he. Jack had been beside her, behind her, under her. He'd done things she'd never dreamed of. He'd made her body sing, made her feel alive and vital. Sex had never been so good.

But it was more than just that, good as Jack was. He'd been tender and loving, too. As she lay in exhaustion, he'd held her and kissed her and told her he'd never known a woman like her.

They'd talked a long time before falling asleep. Jack had surprised her by admitting that he'd miss her when she left. He'd said that in the past, when he'd craved feminine companionship, it hadn't mattered much who the woman was.

"But in the future, when that lonely feeling strikes, that won't be enough," he'd said.

"How do you know?"

"Because you'll be on my mind."

Shelley could tell he'd meant it. At that point he hardly needed to be politic. But his sentimentality did surprise her. "Maybe I shouldn't stay with you," she'd said as she stroked his chest. "Maybe I should stay at Chantal's place. I don't want to make you unhappy."

"It's too late to think of that. I'm already addicted."

"I'm sure you'll be fine. In a couple of weeks you'll have forgotten my name."

He'd smiled. "And if I can still remember it, will you come back to me?"

"Would you like that, really? Two or three visits a year to say hello and get reacquainted. Sounds like a man's thinking to me."

"Wouldn't you enjoy it?"

"Women tend to think of the future differently, in case you haven't noticed. You're the type who lets tomorrow take care of itself. I can tell."

He hadn't argued the point. There'd been no reason to, since they both knew. But instead of dwelling on it, Shelley had given herself up to the moment and to Jack Kincaid. And knowing it was a temporary thing had added to the poignancy and to their fervor.

Sometime during that long night, while she'd been hovering somewhere between ecstasy and sleep, she remembered him saying, "It's going to be strange going back to being chauffeur tomorrow. I think I like you better like this, than when you're playing lady boss."

"What's the matter?" she murmured, as she snuggled against him. "Does it bother you to work for a woman?"

"No, it's not that. I just have a different image of you now. One I like a lot better."

"Just say it, Jack. Like most men, you like women best when they're submitting sexually."

"I go by what feels good. And this feels damned good. I'll admit that much." He'd begun caressing her then, rubbing her all over and making the tremors start once more.

Then, when she was begging for him to take her again, he'd said, "Am I wrong, or does this feel good to you, too?"

It had felt good, all right. But now, by the light of day, the questions he'd raised came back. And despite the warm glow she still felt, Shelley was curious what his attitude would be.

She popped out of bed and went in to shower. When she was dressed she thought she heard Jack's voice in the next room. She went into the sitting room and found him at a small table in the corner where he'd set up his radiotelephone. He was just ending a call and got up to greet her.

"You're looking bright-eyed and bushy-tailed," he said cheerfully.

She went straight into his arms, liking it that Jack seemed to share her need for affection. She wished they could spend the day alone together, but there was work to do. They had to go to Saint Barts so she could talk to the lawyer, Monsieur Voirin, and find out what the story was with Deitz-Langen. Also, she had to meet with Philippe Dufour and make arrangements for turning over her uncle's research.

"Who were you talking to?" she asked.

"Just confirming arrangements for my charter tomorrow. I'm flying a couple of developers from Florida around to look at resort property."

"Plan on bringing them here?" she teased.

"Want to sell?"

"I haven't decided yet."

He gave her a kiss. "I figured as much. How about some breakfast?"

She was grateful for the fact that he was cheerful and wasn't brooding over the lady-boss business. "A cup of coffee does sound good."

They went to the kitchen where Jack had everything ready. "How about if we eat on the terrace?"

They carried everything outside. It was a glorious, balmy morning. The sea looked inviting—not as calm as the night before, but still fairly tranquil under the tropical sun.

"Not to raise an unpleasant subject, but I had a call from Chantal this morning," he said.

"A call?"

"Yeah, she got me on the radio. I guess she didn't want to drive over here and embarrass you again."

"She normally comes over of a morning if she wants to talk?"

"We have breakfast together sometimes," he said with a quirky grin. "But no longer after a night-before."

Shelley hoped that was true. Before, it wouldn't have mattered very much, but in the course of the past twelve hours her feelings toward Jack had changed completely. "So what did she have to say?"

"Claude Perrin has disappeared. When the gendarmes were interviewing everybody yesterday, they were never able to find Claude. She asked me to keep an eye out for him."

"Did you tell her he was here last night?"

"Yes. They assumed he was hiding in the jungle. She said Captain Lasserre has sent to Guadeloupe for someone who can sign so they'll be able to communicate with Claude once they find him. They plan on coming back in force to scour the island, if necessary."

"Poor fellow."

"You didn't seem too charitable toward him last night."

"Well, he scared me. But I'm not at all sure he had bad intentions. I just felt vulnerable and I panicked. That's why I screamed."

"I doubt Claude is mixed up in Henry's murder, but it's up to Lasserre to satisfy himself on the point."

Shelley sipped her coffee. "I'm sure Claude's trying to tell me something. I can't imagine what, though."

"He's probably never seen a little thing as beautiful as you," he said with a wink. "Maybe he wanted to know if you had plans for the evening."

"Oh, Jack, stop thinking with your gonads! If there's a sexual pervert on this island, it's you!"

That brought a burst of laughter. "Last night my perversity didn't seem to matter."

Shelley blushed and got up from the table. "Come on, flyboy, let's get that tin can of yours airborne. I've got business to tend to on Saint Barts."

She started to pick up her dishes, but Jack took her by the wrist and pulled her onto his lap. When she tried to get away, he wouldn't let her.

"You know," she said, "if men weren't bigger and stronger, they'd be at a total loss with women. When all else fails, they try to overpower them."

He kissed her neck. "Let's both be thankful I am bigger and stronger. Otherwise you'd get away and we'd both be lonely."

She pushed against his chest. "You joke, but I think deep down you believe that."

"Honey, I think deep down you believe it, too."

"Oh!" she said, twisting from his grasp and making her escape. "What you lack in social skills, Jack Kincaid, you more than make up for in ego!" Keeping out of his reach, she took her dishes and carried them to the kitchen.

He was roaring with laughter and Shelley smiled in response.

THE FLIGHT ONLY TOOK a few minutes. Though a small island, Saint Barthelemy was well populated, having one good-size town in addition to several villages. Gustavia, the capital, had been built in the colonial era. It was bordered by a protected harbor that had once been filled with trading vessels. Nowadays the port was used by expensive pleasure craft.

Saint Barts had a flourishing tourist industry—though the island had remained relatively unspoiled—and it had become a chic destination for the rich and sophisticated. It boasted a substantial airport, where Jack had his Cessna serviced and fueled.

"I'm taking the opportunity to have some work done on the plane since we'll be spending the day there," Jack told her as they sped over the clear blue water. "I'm flying some big shots around tomorrow and I don't want anything to go wrong."

"What about me?" she asked, her eyes widening. "Am I chopped liver?"

He reached over and took her chin in his hand. "You're a little shot." Then he gave her a kiss. "But then little shots can be the most important of all."

There wasn't much time for flirting. The blue-green profile of Saint Barts loomed ahead. The island was fairly mountainous and, as it turned out, the plane had to slip between two peaks, clearing the saddle between them by little more than thirty feet in order to make the runway, which lay at the base of the mountain. Shelley let out a sigh as they glided down the slope to the concrete landing strip.

"It's kind of exciting the first time," Jack commented after they'd come to a stop. "The trick is to get on the proper glide path and forget the mountain is there."

"Yeah, but what is the passenger supposed to do?"

"Some of them close their eyes," he replied with a laugh.

A customs official met them at the tie-down area. Jack knew the fellow, and when he explained the purpose of their trip, the man took a quick glance at Shelley's passport and handed it back to her. Jack made arrangements for the plane, and they borrowed a *moke* from the mechanic so that they could drive into town to see the lawyer.

Within minutes they were following a road that took them over the saddle they'd just flown over, before twisting down the waterside of the mountain to Gustavia and the sea.

It being summer, there weren't as many tourists as in high season, but the narrow streets of the quaint little town seemed lively enough to Shelley. They parked the *moke* near an open-air vegetable market and walked along the cobbled street.

"Remind me to buy some produce," he said, "so we can have fresh vegetables for dinner. I think I'll get a couple of steaks and a chicken, too."

The primitiveness of Jack's existence hit home again. For him, buying fresh food was an event, a source of pleasure, whereas Shelley had always regarded running to the supermarket as a chore. She realized, now, that there was something appealing about being able to take joy from such a commonplace activity. Without Jack, she never would have made that discovery.

The building they were looking for was at the end of the street, on the corner. It was comparatively new and housed a jewelry store on the ground floor. The lawyer's office was upstairs. Jack told her he didn't know Voirin personally, but believed that the man had a good reputation.

They were greeted by the lawyer himself. Voirin was an austere-looking man in his mid-fifties with blond hair and pale blue eyes. He wore wire-rimmed glasses and a severe expression bordering on a scowl, though his manner was polite.

"I am so happy to make your acquaintance, *madame*," he said, greeting her. "I regarded your late uncle as a friend as well as a client, so it is a pleasure to meet his only family member."

Shelley introduced Jack, whom Voirin seemed to have heard of. "I am glad you are here, Monsieur Kincaid. You'll be interested in what I have to say today, as well."

Jack raised his eyebrows. "Oh?"

"Yes, but please come into my office so we can talk."

Voirin's office was small, but tastefully decorated with antique furniture, old etchings and prints. They settled in their chairs and the lawyer opened the file on his desk.

"As your uncle's *avocat*, Madame Van Dam, I have been charged with the disposition of his estate. I have here his final testament."

"Yes," Shelley said impatiently, "I do want to hear what provisions he made, of course. But if you don't mind, I'd like to discuss Deitz-Langen a moment first. When we spoke on the radiophone, you were concerned that I not give them any of Uncle Henry's research. I'd like to know why?"

"Yes, quite right, *madame*. And forgive me for—how should I say it?—the air of mystery. But as I indicated, the matter is most sensitive."

"I've been really curious, as you can imagine."

"Now that you are here, I shall explain. Your uncle wrote me a letter some months ago, which I have here in the file. You may read it if you like. Monsieur Van Dam believed that he had found a miraculous cure for a variety of neurological diseases. He wanted to license his discovery through the pharmaceutical company that had already done research in that particular field. That company was Deitz-Langen."

"I've already been contacted by their representative, Mr. Baumann," Shelley said.

"I'm not surprised, since they were most interested in the discovery," Voirin replied. "But when your uncle gave them his terms, the Germans balked. You see, Monsieur Van Dam's cure could be manufactured cheaply, and he wanted it marketed at a low price, so anyone who needed the drug could afford it. Deitz-Langen had invested millions of marks in developing their own drugs. The only way for them to recoup that investment was to either get control of your uncle's drug and withhold it from the market, or to offer it at a high price, also."

"So that's the reason they were so eager to get their hands on Uncle Henry's research," Shelley said. "Their fortunes turned on their ability to control the marketing of the discovery."

"So it seems."

She looked at Jack. "They must have been desperate, knowing that Uncle Henry could sell the formula to a competitor."

"Yes," Jack agreed. "But it doesn't make sense that they would kill him without first getting the critical data."

"Your uncle was cognizant of that, *madame*," Voirin explained. "In his letter, he said he was making other arrangements, and that you would be charged with keeping the drug out of Deitz-Langen's hands." The lawyer picked up a three-page letter and passed it across the desk.

Shelley glanced through it, saw that it confirmed what Monsieur Voirin had told her. "Yes," she said, "everything's a lot clearer now—everything except who killed Uncle Henry. But then that's in Captain Lasserre's hands, not mine."

"I've spoken with Lasserre," the lawyer told them. "He wanted to know what I could tell him to help with his investigation. Naturally, I shared everything I could that wasn't confidential."

"Of course," Shelley said, handing back the letter.

"Now, the other matter to discuss is the disposition of the estate," Voirin continued. "I believe you know, *madame*, that you are to receive most of the assets, including the plantation house and the land on Saint Maurice."

"That was what Uncle Henry said he intended to do."

"There is one additional provision. Monsieur Van Dam wanted his discovery in the hands of an expert to be designated by you."

"I'm aware of that. I've already had instructions that Philippe Dufour, my uncle's colleague and good friend, was to receive the materials."

"*Bien, madame,* but did you know that seventy-five percent of the proceeds of sale and future license fees are to stay in the estate for use by your family trust?"

"No, I didn't, though I'm pleased that he wanted something to go to the trust. What happens to the other twenty-five percent?"

"Under the terms of the will, they are to be paid to Monsieur Kincaid."

Shelley turned to Jack, who looked surprised.

"Me?" he said.

"*Oui, monsieur. Vous-même.*"

Jack looked at Shelley, shaking his head with disbelief. "I had no idea. Henry never said a word. I can't imagine why he would be so generous."

"I must tell you, *monsieur,*" Voirin interjected, "Captain Lasserre was asking the same question."

Jack sat nodding his head. "Yeah, and I imagine the bastard figures he's got a motive for murder, too."

"That is not for me to say," the lawyer said.

Shelley had a terrible sinking feeling, and when Jack looked into her eyes, she could tell he was aware of it.

"We're going to have to talk to Lasserre," he said grimly.

She nodded. "Yes, I guess we will."

AFTER THEY LEFT VOIRIN'S office they walked along the dock in silence. Shelley glanced across the harbor at the sea of masts where the sailboats and yachts were moored. A boy on a motorbike passed. The gulls soaring over the harbor cawed at one another like a bunch of angry neighbors.

"I really didn't know about the provision in Henry's will," Jack said after a while. "You believe that, don't you?"

"Of course, I believe you. I wouldn't want to think I spent the night with the man who killed my uncle."

"What you *want* to think is one thing. The question is what you *believe*."

She took his arm, pressing her head against his shoulder. "I know you wouldn't kill him, Jack."

"Then what's bothering you?"

"I'm not sure," she answered with a sigh. "I guess the whole business is starting to get to me. It's like a pit of vipers. Everybody's fighting over Uncle Henry's discovery, when all he wanted was to help mankind. And because of his goodness, he was killed."

Jack walked along without saying anything for a while. "I'd like to point my finger at Karl Baumann and say he or somebody else working for Deitz-Langen killed Henry, but I can't believe they did it. Not without getting hold of the details of Henry's discovery first."

"Maybe he was killed for some other reason," Shelley said. "Deitz-Langen could have been behind the burglary, but not the murder."

"You mean, when they heard Henry was dead, they rushed in to find the research discovery?"

"It's plausible," she replied.

"Yes, and when they didn't find what they were after, they tried to buy it from you."

Shelley brightened. "We'll have to suggest that to Captain Lasserre. Maybe he hasn't thought of that."

"True, but it still doesn't explain why Henry was killed, and that's what Lasserre will be focusing on."

They turned onto the Rue Guadeloupe, then down the street to the gendarmerie, a stucco building flying the French tricolor. They stood in the street in front for a moment before going in.

"I'm afraid," Shelley said.

"Of what?"

"I don't think Captain Lasserre likes you, Jack. I think he's going to try and pin the murder on you."

"It wouldn't surprise me. But no matter, they've abolished capital punishment in France. No more guillotine."

"Don't joke about it."

Jack stroked her cheek with his fingers. "Don't worry, kiddo. After last night, I'd grab you and take off for Brazil before I'd let them put me in jail."

She tried to smile.

"Anyway, I'm only one of several suspects. Lasserre's got to have other names in his hat."

"Let's hope so."

They went inside and Captain Lasserre promptly came out of his office to greet them. He looked even smaller than she'd remembered. His uniform, his mustache and his manner were again impeccable.

"I'm happy to see you both," he said politely.

"We thought since we were in town we'd save you the trouble of arresting me," Jack announced.

"Should I wish to arrest you, Monsieur Kincaid?"

"Mr. Voirin said you'd talked to him."

"Ah," Lasserre replied, "you're referring to your unexpected inheritance."

"Yes, unexpected by me, as well. The first I heard of it was this morning."

"Curious that Monsieur Van Dam would make such a generous gesture and not tell you about it, *n'est-ce pas?*"

"Henry was a curious guy, Captain."

"Indeed. Well, please come into my office."

The three of them entered the captain's Spartan quarters. There were a few trophies, framed pictures of Lasserre and various other officials, plus commendations on the walls. Shelley and Jack sat down on two wooden chairs facing the officer's desk.

"Madame Van Dam," Lasserre began, "I've read through your uncle's notebooks, hoping to discover something that would be useful in my investigation. Unfortunately it's—how do you say?—Greek to me. So I took the liberty of asking Professeur Dufour to assist me. I telephoned him in France and after his arrival this morning he will spend some time looking at the notebooks. I hope this meets with your approval."

"Certainly, Captain Lasserre. I, more than anyone, am interested in finding my uncle's killer."

"Of course," the captain said, nodding politely. He glanced at Jack.

"I am, too," Jack interjected. "Believe it or not."

"You've had some time since we last spoke, *monsieur*. Have you thought of anything else you can suggest that might be helpful?"

"No. Have you turned up anything? Like, for example, what Karl Baumann was doing about the time Henry was killed."

"Thank you for asking. Normally I don't discuss the results of my investigations, but since you were the one who
mentioned Monsieur Baumann, you might as well know
that he was in Europe at the critical time—in France on a
business trip, as a matter of fact. My colleagues in Paris
were able to confirm this."

"How nice for him," Jack observed.

"Too bad you weren't at a meeting yourself that day,
Monsieur Kincaid, instead of out on your boat alone."

"Surely I'm not your only suspect, Captain."

"Is there someone else you care to suggest?"

"Well, Karl Baumann can't be the only person Deitz-
Langen has working on this thing. They could have hired
anyone."

"Quite right, Monsieur Kincaid. And I have given the
matter a great deal of thought after speaking with Monsieur Voirin. There is no question the Germans have a
motive."

"And?"

"One thing troubles me. If Deitz-Langen was involved
in the murder, why would they kill without getting the
critical research first? Additionally, they couldn't have
known that the journals were in safekeeping in California
with Madame Van Dam."

"Whereas I did?" Jack countered. "Is that what you're
suggesting—that as an heir of Henry's, I could safely kill
him because I knew where the research was? I knew, but
the Germans didn't. Isn't that the point?"

"Eloquently stated, *monsieur*. You have a mind for
criminology."

Shelley knew that Lasserre and Jack were jousting, but
the implications had started getting to her.

"This is all speculation," she interrupted. "Anybody
could have killed my uncle for any reason. It didn't nec-

essarily have to be a result of his discovery. Claude Perrin might have murdered him over a mindless disagreement concerning an orchid or something. Even Chantal Favre had a motive. My uncle wouldn't agree to her plans to develop the island. Or Simone Roche might have fought with him over some vegetable or a dispute over pay. I'm not accusing anyone, but talk is cheap. I haven't known Jack long, Captain Lasserre, but if you want my opinion, I don't believe he's capable of killing for money or anything else."

"Perhaps you aren't as objective, *madame*, as you would like to appear."

Shelley's eyes flashed. "What is that supposed to mean?"

Jack patted her arm. "That's all right, Shelley, I think all the captain is saying is that your standards for judging are not the same as his."

"And his are better?"

"They're the ones the courts listen to."

She looked at Jack with disbelief. "Whose side are you on, anyway?"

"Yours, of course. The fact is, Captain Lasserre doesn't have enough to charge me. I know it and he knows it. But just so that he doesn't get too frustrated, it would be nice if the real killer turned up."

"You are very confident, *monsieur*," the policeman said. "The mark of a man who is either foolhardy, or innocent."

"I like to think I'm not a fool."

"Just so. But fact, not sentiment, is what matters." Lasserre turned to Shelley. "True, *madame?*"

She gave him a steely look. "Jack's neither a killer nor a fool."

"I admire your confidence, *madame*. Hopefully it will be rewarded." The gendarme looked back and forth at the two of them. "I trust you both understand I am only doing my duty. I am not accusing anyone at this point. My investigation is only beginning. My interest in the Germans continues. They certainly have a compelling motive."

"If they were involved, they would have to have been on Saint Maurice on those critical days when the murder and burglary occurred," Jack said. "Doing that unseen is not easy. Have you looked at that angle, Captain?"

"Excellent, Monsieur Kincaid! If you tire of being a pilot, you might take up police work. As a matter of fact, we are in the process of checking plane and boat charters throughout the Caribbean."

"Any luck?"

"Nothing under the name Deitz-Langen, yet. However, a German travel agency arranged some boat charters out of Saint Martin last month. We aren't sure of the exact dates yet or the principals involved, but we are looking into it."

"Then there's hope you'll uncover the real villain."

"It's never a pleasure for the police to see an innocent man convicted, *monsieur*, I assure you. We much prefer to catch the real thief."

"I'm glad you two can take this so lightly," Shelley commented.

"My work is often grim, *madame*," Lasserre replied. "One must do what one can to retain one's sanity." He smiled at Jack, then turned back to her. "The important point, *madame*, is that we are not quite ready to send your . . . pilot . . . to the guillotine."

Shelley looked at Jack, who glanced at his watch.

"We've got some time to kill before we have to pick up Dufour at the airport," he said insouciantly. "Want to do a little shopping? There're some great stores here."

Shelley's mouth dropped open and both Jack and Lasserre laughed. She got to her feet and, slinging her purse over her shoulder, headed out of the room. "Men!" she exclaimed.

11

SHELLEY AND JACK SAT under the overhanging roof at the back of the terminal building, waiting for Philippe Dufour's plane to arrive from Guadeloupe. She mulled over the events of the past few days.

Once Captain Lasserre had assured himself that there was nothing in the journals important to the murder investigation, she'd be able to turn them over to Professor Dufour. That would relieve her of her most pressing responsibility. Then, all she would have left would be the disposal of the plantation house and any personal property. Chantal Favre would certainly help her with that task, but Shelley still wasn't comfortable with a solution her uncle had opposed.

"Jack," she said, "what would you think if I decided to hang on to Uncle Henry's place for a while?"

"You mean keep it as a second home? For vacations?"

She shook her head. "No, I mean delay my decision. There's nothing that says I have to do anything with it now."

"That would mean coming back, probably."

"Would you like that?"

He took her hand and rubbed it against his cheek and said, "It would be nice if you never left. It's kind of pleasant having you around."

"You aren't getting sentimental on me, are you?"

"Don't make fun," he said, sounding serious. "I mean it."

"One night together and you've decided you want me to stick around?"

He kissed her fingers. "It was a long night."

Shelley laughed.

"You shouldn't make light of it."

"What? This from a man who jokes with the police about going to the guillotine?"

Jack gave her a crooked grin. "Some things are important and others aren't."

She cuffed him playfully. "Jack Kincaid, I may not have known you very long, but I know you well enough to know you're full of it."

He shrugged. "What can I say?"

Shelley watched as a single-engine plane suddenly appeared between the two peaks and glided smoothly down to the runway. She glanced at Jack out of the corner of her eye. He sat there with a thoughtful, vaguely sad look on his face. It occurred to her that maybe the sentimentality he'd expressed was genuine.

All day, flashes of the night before had drifted through her mind. It took a real effort to look at Jack without recalling their lovemaking, the feel of his chest against her breasts or the taste of his mouth. But she'd tried to focus on the business at hand. After all, at best Jack was a pleasant distraction. She couldn't allow herself to think he might be more than that.

"That may be the professor's plane," Jack said, pointing to a larger two-engine aircraft that was gliding down over the slope of the mountain and nearing the runway. Within minutes the plane was taxiing toward the terminal building. Jack and Shelley got up.

"You've seen the professor before, haven't you?" she asked.

"Yeah, I flew him in when he visited Henry."

The passengers were soon disembarking, most of them French and in resort wear. One of the last off the plane was a rather disheveled-looking man of sixty in a tropical-weight suit and Panama hat. Jack didn't have to tell her that it was Philippe Dufour.

The professor was of medium height and carried a briefcase. When he got close, Shelley could see he had a white goatee and his hair was thin and shaggy. He was squinting through his glasses at the brightness of the sun as he followed the other passengers toward the terminal building.

Shelley intercepted him, extending her hand. "Professor Dufour, I'm Shelley Van Dam."

Dufour removed his hat, revealing a nearly bald dome. He shook her hand energetically. *"Enchanté, madame,"* he said, grinning. *"Enchanté."*

"You remember Jack Kincaid," she said, introducing Jack.

"Certainement. Bonjour, Monsieur Kincaid." He shook Jack's hand, then turned back to Shelley. "Let me say, *madame,* how very sad I am at the passing of your uncle. He was a dear friend. My sincere condolences."

"Thank you, Professor. And now the tragedy has been compounded by the news that he was murdered. I assume you've heard."

Dufour made a tsking sound and nodded. "Yes, I was told by the gendarmes. *Tragique.*"

They went toward the entrance to the building. "Did you have a good flight?" Shelley asked as they walked.

"From Guadeloupe not so bad," the professor replied. "But yesterday from Paris . . . Ooof! When you are old the long flights are . . . terrible."

Dufour's scattered, eccentric personality made Shelley smile. But it also made her a bit melancholy, because in a way he reminded her of her uncle.

"Perhaps you'd like some lunch, Professor, before we go to the gendarmerie," Jack suggested.

"Oh, no. If you don't mind, I'd like to see Henry's journals straightaway. I spoke with the captain and he asked for my help in interpreting them. And I am most interested in seeing what Henry was up to, as you say."

They got the Frenchman's baggage and Jack carried the case to the *moke*, which was parked nearby. Shelley climbed in back and they took off up the hill with the professor holding on to his Panama hat so that it wouldn't blow off in the wind.

Shelley leaned forward between the men to speak. "Professor Dufour, did my uncle ever tell you about the problems he'd had with Deitz-Langen?"

"I was aware, yes," he answered hesitantly.

"Based on what we've been told, Uncle Henry's discovery could have cost them millions. Jack and I think it's connected with the murder in some way."

"What makes you say it would cost them millions? Where did you learn this?"

"We found out just today, as a matter of fact. From Uncle Henry's lawyer. He had a letter from my uncle explaining why Deitz-Langen should not receive the research."

"I wasn't aware of the letter, but I shouldn't be surprised Henry wrote it."

"Henry seems to have spread bits and pieces of the puzzle around to a variety of people," Jack said. "Do you have any idea what the discovery was, Professor?"

"No. Only that its benefits were to the neurological system. It is most effective with certain diseases and disorders and, according to Henry, very cheap to—how do you say?—*fabriquer?*"

"Manufacture," Jack explained.

"Yes, manufacture. This is very important."

They were on the part of the road that twisted down to Gustavia now. Philippe Dufour was still hanging on to his hat. He glanced back at Shelley.

"Tell me, *madame*," he said, "how do you feel about the marketing of Henry's miracle drug?"

"What do you mean?"

"Do you have the same prejudices as your uncle?"

"I don't know about prejudices," she replied, "but I feel Uncle Henry's wishes should be honored. He felt his discovery should be available at minimal cost to those who need it, and I think he was right."

"I see."

"Don't you, Professor?"

"Naturally I will do as Henry wished."

Shelley liked his response. "I'll certainly be glad when everything is in your hands," she told him. "The responsibility has proved to be a real burden."

"I shall do my duty," Philippe Dufour said. "Be assured, *madame*."

THEY DROPPED the professor at the gendarmerie and agreed to return in a few hours. Then Jack suggested they go to one of his favorite places for lunch. They drove across the mountain ridge, through a village and past fields that had been cleared for pasture before arriving at the Baie des Flamands. Finally, off a palm-lined side drive, they came to a group of cottages at the edge of the beach.

"This is the Taiwana, a sort of hotel-restaurant," he said. "A friend of mine runs the place."

Food was served on a terrace covered by a thatched roof. Jack picked a table with a view of the breakers rolling in off the Atlantic. There was a flower garden nearby and the air was fragrant with the scent of blossoms and the sea.

They chose the special, a *salade niçoise*, and a glass of wine. The waitress, a lovely girl who looked to be of Tahitian and French blood, seemed to know Jack rather well. He spoke only French to her, so Shelley wasn't always sure what was being said.

Once they were alone again, she noticed Jack was gazing at her. He smiled and she smiled. She had a sudden flash of what he was all about, his carefree life of going from one woman to the next. She'd been alone with him most of the time, except when Chantal was around. He'd explained her away, but the truth was, Chantal was only one of many.

"By the look on your face, I can tell what you're thinking," he said.

"Oh?"

"That I've got a girl in every port."

His insight surprised her. "*Do* you have someone in every port, Jack?"

"I live the life of a bachelor. I don't have a wife and kiddies at home. Nor do I live like a man who does. I make no apologies for that."

"I wasn't suggesting that you should."

"Maybe, but the disapproval on your face is undeniable."

She squirmed a bit. "You're different from the other men I've dated, Jack, and that makes it hard for me to understand my feelings." She drew a long breath, maintaining eye contact. "I'll admit I'm very attracted to you—that's pretty obvious. But it's not just the physical part that attracts me, and that's why I'm so confused."

He grinned wryly. "It's nice to know I'm not the only one."

"Who's confused, you mean?"

"No, who's surprised by this . . . thing . . . between us."

His understanding came as a relief. "I suppose it's a sort of infatuation." She flushed at her own words when she realized what she'd said.

"Meaningless, in other words."

She fought back the flush in her cheeks. "I don't know about meaningless."

"Well, are you . . . slumming? Having a fling for the hell of it?"

"Of course not."

"But you think I'm only out for a good time," he said.

"I'm not suggesting that at all. It's just that when you're used to a certain type of person, and you find yourself attracted to somebody so completely different . . . it's a little scary."

Jack reached across the table and took her hand. "Would it help any if I told you my feelings scare me a little, too? It works both ways, you know."

"You really feel that way, Jack?"

"When I first saw you, I had you pegged as a drill sergeant. You were like a little bulldog nipping at my heels. It was good entertainment. But now that I've seen your softer side, it's not so easy to be blasé."

It was vintage Jack Kincaid, but she was beginning to like it—a lot, if she was honest. Everything about him was starting to appeal to her. It felt good just to be with him, to live the way he lived. That was frightening, because they weren't living in her world, they were in his.

Jack ran his knuckle under his mustache, studying her.

"What are you thinking?" she asked.

"I was trying to imagine how you'd have reacted to me if we'd met in L.A. instead of here."

"Well, if you were hanging out in some nautical bar in Venice Beach and you had a gold chain around your neck and you were trying to hit on all the twenty-year-old waitresses, I wouldn't be interested in giving you a shot."

"But say I was just me. Like I am. Boom! Beamed down right in the middle of Santa Monica."

Shelley leaned on the table, resting her chin in her hand. "I can't picture you in L.A., Jack. Try as I may, I can't do it."

"Obviously a defense mechanism of some sort."

She laughed.

"Well, my dear, since I'm not the gold-chain type, you'll have to take me as you find me. After lunch why don't I see if the manager still has an old chess set kicking around? If you're up to it, I could give you another lesson."

She smiled. "Are you trying to say you're interested in my mind as well as my body?"

"Could be."

The waitress came with their soup. "Let me ask *you* something, Jack," Shelley said as the waitress set a soup bowl in front of her.

"Yes?"

"If I was one of your party girls, and you brought me here for lunch, would you suggest we take a room afterward?"

Jack glanced up at the waitress, who brushed back her long black hair and acted oblivious to them. Shelley couldn't tell whether she understood what they were saying or not. He paused for a moment, then said, "That's a tricky question."

"No trickier than yours."

"All right," he admitted, "the answer is there's a good chance that I would, yes."

"I thought so."

"You should be flattered that I treat you differently, Shelley."

"Why?"

The waitress left them without a word.

"Because you're in a class by yourself."

She laughed sardonically. "You mean I'm the one woman you'd rather play chess with?"

"The one woman I'd rather spend time with," Jack replied, as he picked up his soup spoon. He gave her a sly look. *"Bon appétit,* my dear."

WHEN HE WON HIS FIRST pawn and Shelley gave him a look worthy of a scrappy street fighter, he knew this was a woman who would be next to impossible to get out of his mind. Ten moves later he won his second pawn, and began wondering if he was falling in love with her. By the time she turned her king over on its side, he was pretty sure he was.

"Well," Shelley said, "at least I learn when I lose to you."

"I learned a lot in that game myself."

"Oh? What?"

"It's a subject for another time. How about a walk on the beach before we head back to town?"

"I'd like that."

They got up and stepped right off the terrace and onto the sand. Shelley kicked off her sandals and spun around, her skirt swirling. She looked more carefree and joyful than he'd seen her since they'd met. Could she feel the same way he did?

He took her hand as they headed across the broad sandy beach. There were a few villas and another hotel farther around the bay, and so there were a dozen or so sunbathers scattered along the beach. Among them was a couple of shapely beauties—topless—though he hardly noticed. Shelley Van Dam had really gotten to him; she was no ordinary woman.

When they returned to the Taiwana, it was time to go back to town. Jack could tell she was as regretful as he that their jaunt was ending. They could have happily stayed at the Taiwana for hours, playing chess, walking, talking, eating, just being together.

"That was delightful," Shelley said as they climbed into the *moke*. "I'd like to come here again."

"If you return to Saint Maurice for a visit sometime, I'll bring you back." It almost seemed sacrilegious to suggest they'd ever be apart, but he knew that was the reality, even though he hadn't wanted to think about it. And the deeper his feelings for her got, the more troubling that thought became.

"You know the worst part about talking about coming back?" she asked.

"What?"

"Knowing it means I'll have to go."

"Yes," he said as he started the engine. "I was thinking the same thing."

They didn't talk much on their way back to Gustavia. And instead of enjoying the sights, Shelley stared wistfully out of the *moke*, letting the wind blow her hair.

Jack was drawn to that image of her, though she seemed to have become a bit melancholy. He liked it better when she was cheerful and full of life, or even when she was being combative. And he wondered if she was beginning to be sad at the thought of leaving him.

When they arrived at the gendarmerie, Captain Lasserre and the professor were waiting, both looking rather grim. Philippe Dufour was seated at a large table with Henry's notebooks piled all around him. The policeman stood behind the professor.

"I'm afraid there's troubling news," Lasserre announced, his eyes hard with accusation. "A critical page from the journal is missing."

"What?" Shelley exclaimed.

The professor shook his head, seeming genuinely distressed. "I haven't had time to read through all the notebooks, but I've looked carefully at the one that seems to contain the most information on Henry's great medical discovery."

"And?"

"He describes the drug in detail. The active ingredient is extracted from an exotic plant, that much is made clear."

"So what's the problem?" Jack asked.

"The problem, *monsieur*," Philippe Dufour replied, "is that the page on which the plant is named has been torn from the notebook. All other references in the journals are to 'the plant' or 'the specimen,' but the scientific designation is repeated nowhere."

"What are you suggesting?" Shelley demanded. "That it's been stolen?"

"There is no question about it," Captain Lasserre said. "What I wish to know is who removed it."

"I gather you have some nominees," Jack suggested.

Lasserre drew himself up. "The list is short, *monsieur*. Henry Van Dam sent the notebooks to his niece. She returned them to Saint Maurice, placing them in your custody. I took them from you, *monsieur*, and they've been locked away ever since. The professor has examined them in my presence, or in the presence of one of my associates. Perhaps you would like to offer a theory."

"It doesn't mean that one of us took it," Shelley pointed out. "The suitcase was sitting unguarded for hours at a time in both the plantation house and Jack's cottage. There was plenty of opportunity for someone to steal the missing page."

"I've considered that possibility, *madame*," the captain replied. "And I've discussed it with Professor Dufour. It seems unlikely that the page was taken in such a fashion. The thief would have to know exactly what he wanted and where to look in the journals. The professor here is very familiar with Monsieur Van Dam's work. Yet it took him over an hour to locate the critical material. For an ordinary thief, the task would have been impossible."

"Jack and I may have had the time for a careful search, but what makes you think we would know where to look, much less recognize the critical material if we saw it?" Shelley asked.

"I am accusing no one, *madame*," Lasserre declared. "But it seems evident that the page was removed by someone with an opportunity and sufficient time to do the job. I cannot suggest another besides we four in this room."

"You're overlooking one other possible suspect, Captain," Jack said.

"Oh? Who would that be, *monsieur*?"

"Henry."

"Monsieur Van Dam? But why? The notebooks were his."

"That's perfectly consistent with his way of doing things," Jack said. "Henry parceled bits of information out to everybody. If you think about it, nearly everyone he's dealt with knows something. Consider the list. There's Shelley, of course, and me. Professor Dufour had some knowledge of Henry's work. But important information was also put in Chantal Favre's hands, as well as Henry's lawyer, Monsieur Voirin. Why wouldn't Henry take the one critical page from the journals and give it to yet another person for safekeeping, complicating the puzzle one step further?"

"But who?" Philippe Dufour asked gloomily.

Lasserre smiled ironically at Jack. "You're very clever, *monsieur*. I must confess your idea never occurred to me. Be aware though, it could also be an inventive diversion. If I were a large pharmaceutical company after special information, I would enlist the assistance of a person with access to steal the material I wanted."

"Someone like me, in other words," Jack said.

Lasserre shrugged.

"I suppose you're entitled to your theories as much as I am," Jack told the captain, "but a large pharmaceutical company could do business with a policeman every bit as easily as with a pilot. And if I'm not mistaken, the journals were here just as long as they were in my house."

Captain Lasserre turned scarlet. "And what next, Monsieur Kincaid? Are you going to suggest that *I* killed Henry Van Dam?"

"Jack's not suggesting anything," Shelley cut in. "He's only pointing out that there's no proof against him or anyone else."

"Still, *madame*, there is a question of honor."

"It may all be for nothing," she replied, brushing the captain's comment aside. "Jack might be right. Uncle Henry may have torn the page out of the notebook himself. Or it could be that the burglars found both the page and a plant specimen and are happily enjoying the fruits of their crime."

"Regardless, there remains a murderer to unmask," Captain Lasserre declared, with a biting glare at Jack.

"Shelley," Jack said, "I think it's time to go. Unless, of course, the good captain proposes to make an arrest."

"You will be the first to know, *monsieur*," the gendarme returned scathingly.

Shelley took Jack's arm. "I agree, it's time to leave." She smiled, trying to lighten the mood. "What about the journals, Professor? Are they useless with the page missing?"

"No, *madame*, not at all. There is a wealth of data here. And I may be able to figure out Henry's secret by putting together other information. But it will require hours of work."

Shelley turned to Lasserre. "May the professor take my uncle's journals now, Captain?"

"For the moment, I should like to keep them here. I have no objection if Professor Dufour would like to continue to study them, however." He glanced at Jack. "I am still hopeful that a clue to the identity of the killer will be found in them."

"All right," Shelley agreed, pulling on Jack's arm. "We'll be on Saint Maurice if you need us. Goodbye, gentlemen." She dragged Jack toward the door.

They were no sooner in the street when Shelley stopped and put her hands on her hips. "Jack Kincaid, unless you learn to keep your mouth shut, they're going to bring the guillotine out of retirement just for you."

He laughed, liking her this way better than sad. "Lasserre is looking for a scapegoat, honey, that's all. God knows why he picked me, unless his wife had an affair with a pilot once."

Shelley gave him a suspicious look, but apparently decided not to ask. Jack was relieved because he didn't want to get into the subject of his past again. She took his arm and they headed for the *moke*.

"I think I want to go home," she said.

"You weren't impressed by the captain's theory that I'm in cahoots with the bad guys?"

"No. To be honest, I think your theory makes more sense. It's in keeping with Uncle Henry's way of doing things. The question is, who would he have given that page to?"

"He might have kept it, as you suggested to Lasserre. And you're right, Shelley. It could have been stolen later—either when Henry was killed, or at the time of the burglary. Throwing that into the pot was pretty clever, by the way."

They came to the *moke*. "I was just trying to get Lasserre off your back," she said, climbing into the vehicle. "I think the page is around somewhere, undiscovered. Otherwise Deitz-Langen wouldn't still be after Uncle Henry's research."

"That visit could have been a diversion to cover up what they'd already done," Jack suggested.

"But what if I'd taken Karl Baumann's offer of five million? It would have been an expensive cover-up to get hold of some notebooks that were probably worthless."

"It's a damned complicated situation," Jack commented as he started the engine. "And you want to know something? I think Henry would have been pleased about all the trouble he's caused."

She nodded. "I think you're right."

"Before we head for the airport we've got some very important business to tend to."

"What's that?"

"We have to go to the market and do our grocery shopping. I have a special dinner planned for tonight."

THE SUN WAS GETTING LOW by the time they made it back to Saint Maurice. This time Shelley didn't close her eyes as the plane skimmed the treetops and settled on the little airstrip. She had confidence in Jack Kincaid—in nearly every respect.

Jack told her he always enjoyed the walk from the strip back to his house. It was a pleasant way to reimmerse himself in the tranquillity of Saint Maurice, especially after the hassle of the airports and traffic on the larger islands.

"You mean the dizzying pace of a metropolis like Charlotte Amalie or Gustavia?" she said with a laugh.

Jack put his arm around her shoulder as they walked along the trail. "Everything is relative, my dear. That's one truism I've come to know with certainty."

"I'd like to see you in L.A.," she said.

"Oh, God."

"I'm serious. I'll bet you'd do better than you think. You could appreciate the good things—the culture, the restaurants, the creature comforts—and still manage to keep it all in perspective. I know you could."

"Hey, are you with the chamber of commerce or something?"

She jabbed him in the ribs. "Wouldn't you visit me in L.A. sometime if I invited you?"

"Why? So you could see me outside my natural habitat?"

"Jack!" She stopped dead in her tracks, folding her arms over her chest. "Maybe that *is* why. Maybe I'd like to sit at *my* dining-room table with you, so I could see how it feels to be with you in *my* natural surroundings. Maybe I'd like to walk on the beach at Malibu with you, or go to the Getty museum just to see what it would be like. Is that so bad?"

Jack lowered his eyes.

Shelley suddenly felt stupid. She couldn't have been much more blatant. "Oh, never mind," she said. "Forget I mentioned it." She took off up the trail at a rapid pace—anything to get away. The faster she walked, the more embarrassed she became.

Pretty soon Jack was alongside her, pacing her, stride for stride. She tried to ignore him.

"Listen, Shelley," he said, "I didn't say I wouldn't come to L.A. As a matter of fact, I'm flattered that you asked—"

"Oh, forget it! You're only making things worse."

He took hold of her arm then and stopped her. She tried to jerk free, but he kept a tight grip. He set the bag of groceries down, taking hold of her with both hands.

"Don't pull the big macho act with me," she snapped. "You don't have on a gold chain." She pulled herself free and glared at him, really angry, though as much with herself as with him. Jack just smiled and that really made her steam. "And so help me," she went on, shaking a finger, "if you say something inane, like I'm really beautiful when I'm angry, I'm going to belt you, Jack Kincaid. I'm warning you!"

He gave her a look and shrugged. "But it's true!"

She swung at him but he grabbed her wrist. Jack didn't act the least concerned. He seemed to be enjoying every minute of their little game. When she tried to squirm out of his grasp, he simply pulled her against him and held her tightly.

"Truce?" he whispered.

Shelley looked up into his eyes, knowing he was going to kiss her. All day long she'd been waiting for when he would. He'd played it pretty straight till now, keeping things professional, except when he'd taken her hand or given her an intimate smile. But now they were alone. There was no need for more pretense.

Jack took her chin in his hand, then lifted her face and kissed her tenderly. It wasn't a very long kiss, but it set her heart to pounding. Maybe it was the expectation that did it to her.

When the kiss finally ended, she melted into his embrace, her eyes closed, recollections of all those wonderful sensations from the night before going through her mind. Then she opened her eyes and found him smiling down at her. The conquering hero.

Hard as she tried, Shelley just couldn't be angry. A part of her *wanted* to be conquered. Yet there was another part of her that didn't want his victory to come too easily. Giving him an indifferent shrug, she turned and started along the trail.

Jack walked beside her, not saying a word. Finally, when she didn't speak, he said, "What are you thinking, Shelley?"

"I was thinking about who should make dinner."

"Is that all?"

"No. I was also hoping you might have another chessboard around your house. I'm in the mood to give you a real shellacking."

He chuckled. "You know what I love about you?"

"What?"

"You're not a very good loser."

"Know why that is, Kincaid?"

"No, why?"

"Because I never lose for long."

12

JACK BARBECUED THE steaks while Shelley made the rest of the dinner. He dug out an excellent Bordeaux, which they drank with their meal. They talked and ate, sipped wine and laughed. She couldn't remember ever feeling so content.

After they'd finished dinner, they sat outside on the patio, finishing their wine. Shelley felt lighthearted and happy. "This trip might spoil me for life," she said wistfully.

"How so?"

"I cringe at the thought of driving down a freeway now."

"Maybe you should stay here, then," he told her.

"So that I'd have only one vehicle to dodge?"

"There'd be other advantages," Jack replied, taking her hand and kissing her fingers.

"I'd tell you how tempting you are, Jack, but your ego's had plenty of stroking already."

"A man can never get too much stroking."

"Yes," she agreed. "I've learned that in my twenty-nine years. Men are the most egocentric creatures alive."

"It's a source of strength."

"It's also your Achilles' heel."

"What makes you say that?" he asked.

"Get out your chess set and I'll show you."

Jack laughed. "One quick game."

"Why only one?"

"I've got other plans for the evening."

"Then you'd better lose."

"No," he said, shaking his head. "My ego would never allow that."

"Precisely my point."

Jack gave her a sly look and went inside. He came back a few moments later with a folding chessboard and a small box of chessmen.

"This isn't Uncle Henry's set," she said.

"No, it's mine."

"I want to beat you the first time with Uncle Henry's pieces."

"All right." Jack went back inside and returned with the set that Shelley had given him. "Be warned," he said, opening the box. "I'm merciless, whatever set we use."

"Your days are numbered, Jack Kincaid."

Shelley surprised him and won a pawn in the opening. She fought hard through the middle game, nearly winning a bishop, but Jack managed to overcome her advantage, beating her in a drawn-out endgame.

"Damn," she said, when it became hopeless and she had to resign. "I thought for sure I had you this time."

"I was beginning to think so myself," he admitted.

Shelley leaned back, running her fingers through her hair. "I enjoy our games," she said, stretching. "I enjoy them a lot."

Jack's expression softened as he studied her. Gone was the look of the fierce competitor. His gaze was admiring now. "How about a walk before bed?" he said. "The moonlight is bright."

"I'd enjoy that."

There was a path that continued on along the shore, and they took that to the next promontory, a rocky point a hundred yards or so beyond the cottage. From there they could look northeast into the Atlantic. The ocean was dark with hardly a ship to be seen. Jack had his arm around her and she hugged him as she looked up at the sequined sky.

"I'll miss Saint Maurice," she said.

"And I'll miss you."

He kissed her then, and Shelley became very emotional. She wasn't entirely sure if she felt good or bad, whether being with Jack was a blessing or a curse. A sudden feeling of insecurity went through her. She was afraid of loving him too much. "I think I want to go back," she whispered.

He didn't object. They made their way along the dark path. Back at the cottage, Jack lit a candle and they went into the bedroom. Shelley sat on the bed. He put down the candle and stared at her in the flickering shadows.

"Why so sad?" he asked.

A tear rolled down her cheek. She wiped it away. "Maybe I'm sorry I lost that game."

Jack sat beside her. "Somehow I don't think that's it." He kissed her cheek.

The tears started flowing. She wasn't even sure why. Maybe the emotion of the past few days had caught up with her. Or maybe it was Jack. "Damn you," she murmured.

"What have I done?"

"I like being with you. Too much. That's what you've done."

"That's a hard one for me to rectify."

"I know. I'm being silly and emotional. I'm sorry."

He kissed her lips. It aroused her. The whole day had been building to this moment, though neither of them had rushed toward it.

Soon Jack's fingers were digging into her flesh. He became aroused as quickly as she, his breathing heavy and determined. When the kiss ended, her body was warm and desirous. Jack slowly began unbuttoning her blouse, then helped her out of it.

Shelley felt strange and wonderful despite the lingering sadness. She wanted to be with him, wanted him to hold her.

He unhooked her bra and pushed it away so he could kiss her nipples until they were throbbing. Then he made her stand before him so that he could remove her skirt. After he'd pulled down her panties, she was naked. She didn't feel shy; she felt alive and ready for his affection.

Jack ran his hands down her sides, caressing her. He cupped her buttocks and pulled her against him, burying his face in the soft mounds of her breasts.

He drew his hand between her legs until his fingers met her moist center. She moaned. "Oh God, Jack, you excite me so."

He got up, pulling back the covers so that she could get into bed, then bent down and began nibbling a trail from her breasts to her knees. He drew his tongue up the inside of her thigh and pressed his face into her. Shelley parted her legs to let him kiss her more fully. The excitement nearly overwhelmed her. In seconds she was on the verge of climax. She tried to stop him, because she didn't want to come—not yet, not without him inside her. But Jack wouldn't stop. He caressed her with his tongue until she couldn't hold back anymore. Helpless to prevent it, she climaxed violently, her body heaving as surges of ecstasy coursed through her.

Afterward she lay panting, the pulsing so strong that it was almost painful. She could only moan, her eyes closed, her body tingling.

Eventually the feeling began to subside and fatigue replaced the excitement. She'd been so caught up in her pleasure that she'd hardly been aware of Jack. Opening her eyes, she saw him standing beside her, unbuttoning his shirt.

Though she had been completely satisfied only minutes earlier, watching him undress began to arouse her again. And this time her craving for him was even more intense.

When he was naked, she ached for him to take her.

Jack climbed onto the bed then and Shelley parted her legs to receive him. Guiding him into her moist center, she arched her hips to make the penetration complete. He had barely started to move against her when her excitement rose once more toward climax. But his movements were slow and deliberate, forcing her to hold back.

"Oh, Shelley," he murmured, "I want you so badly. I can hardly stand it."

"Please," she moaned. "Now."

Suddenly he stopped, their bodies completely entwined, his penetration complete. His face hovered over hers. She looked into his eyes as the shadows in the room danced around them.

"I love you, Shelley," he whispered. "I love you so very much. I want you to know that."

She began to cry. Pulling his face down to hers, she kissed him. Jack began to rock against her, his rhythm rapidly quickening. Within seconds they both came.

She clung to him afterward, feeling pleasure, joy, sadness—all at once.

For a long, long time they lay motionless. When she heard him whisper again that he loved her, she was already halfway asleep.

Did she tell him that she loved him, too, or was it in her dream? Did she say she wanted to stay with him always, or was that only in her imagination? She fell into a deep sleep with her body still cleaved to his. All she knew was that was the way she wanted to stay—forever if possible.

JACK'S ALARM WENT OFF just before dawn. He had his arm over her and they both jumped at the sound. After turning off the alarm, he embraced her again, gathering her close.

"Believe it or not, I've got to go to work," he mumbled.

Shelley was too comfortable, was still feeling too fulfilled, to move. Jack got up and she was vaguely aware of the sound of the shower, but she fell asleep until sometime later when he returned to her, smelling of tangy cologne and toothpaste.

"I've got to go, kiddo. Will you be all right?"

She nodded, still half asleep. "Yes, fine."

"I'll be back late afternoon."

"Uh-huh."

"There's coffee in the kitchen."

"Uh-huh."

"Will you be a good girl while I'm gone?"

"Uh-huh."

He kissed her. It was only then that she realized he was leaving.

"Jack," she called, as he was about to go out the door.

"Yes?"

"I'll miss you."

"I'll miss you, too, honey."

"Be careful."

He blew her a kiss, then left. For a while she lay in bed, though she never really went back to sleep. Thoughts of Jack kept her awake. She was in love with a man she would be leaving soon.

Shelley got up and slipped on a T-shirt and a pair of shorts. As she was walking through the front room, she heard the sound of Jack's plane and ran out onto the terrace. Just then he came roaring by, a few hundred feet above the cottage. Shelley waved. He tipped his wings as he headed out across the sea toward Saint Martin.

She watched the plane until it was a speck melting into the horizon. Going back inside, she saw the chess set on the table. Smiling at the memory of their game, she began putting the pieces in the box. She started to pick up the board, and Jack's set, too, when on an impulse she decided to have a look and see what his pieces were like.

She opened the box and found a sheet of paper. When she unfolded it, her mouth dropped open. It was a scientific drawing of an exotic plant, neatly labeled in her uncle's meticulous hand. It was the missing page from the journals.

Oh, my God, she thought. Then she noted another scrap of paper in the box. It was a note, also in her uncle's hand.

Jack,
I'm leaving this important piece of my research with you for safekeeping. I fear for my life and for the sanctity of my work. The plant described herein is key to a pharmacological discovery of the utmost importance. A specimen is hidden among those in my collection. Should anything happen to me, see that this paper and the specimen get into the hands of my niece. If you happen to find this before the plant is delivered to those I trust, guard the secret, I beg you.
                                                          Henry

Jack had been right: Henry had torn the page out of the notebook himself! Shelley sighed with relief. She read the note a second time, then realized that the specimen was still missing. Was it at the plantation house, or had it been taken by someone? The burglars, perhaps?

Shelley tried to picture the solarium, but couldn't recall a plant resembling the one in the drawing. But she had to find out if it was still there, or if it had been taken. She'd go up to the house and look for it.

Taking the drawing with her, Shelley headed for the plantation house.

It had been a couple of days since she'd been inside and the air seemed stale. There was a heavy silence, too, making her nervous. She was sorry Jack wasn't with her. She walked through the house, tiptoeing, though it wasn't necessary. Some of her things were upstairs, but the place felt alien. Home was with Jack now.

She went into the laboratory. The large group of plants that had been on a table in the middle of the room was still there, undisturbed. Nothing resembling the specimen was evident, but she wanted to make sure. She examined each plant closely. None resembled the one in the drawing. Maybe it had been stolen.

Her expectation turned to disappointment. But then she thought of the compost pile in back. Suddenly she heard a rustling sound. Turning, she saw a man rise from behind the table. His face was dark and dirty and hideous. Unable to help herself, she screamed.

Claude stood there, staring at her, looking as frightened as she was. Shelley managed to regain her composure. Glancing at his feet she saw a blanket and some rags. She realized that he'd been sleeping on the floor. While the villagers searched the jungle for him, he'd been hiding in the home of his only friend.

Claude seemed to recover from the shock of their encounter, as well. Making strange little sounds, he extended his hand and started moving toward her, just as he had at Jack's. Trembling, Shelley reached for the door handle. Should she run? Did he mean her harm?

She went outside, but Claude was right on her heels. He took her arm, and started pulling her around the house, just as he had that other time.

Unsure what he was up to, she didn't resist. Better to wait and see. They walked along the side of the house and stopped at the library window. Claude pointed inside. Then the poor man became very agitated, again making his strange sounds, and gesticulating.

"I don't understand, Claude," she said, shaking her head.

He rolled his eyes heavenward and looked as if he were going to cry. Then he reached into his coat pocket and took out the photo of Henry he'd shown her before. Claude pointed to her uncle, then into the library. When she still didn't understand, he pointed to his own eye, then at Henry, then into the library.

"You saw Uncle Henry in the library," she prompted.

Then Claude took an imaginary object in his hands, lifted it over his head and brought it down sharply, pointing once more at the picture of her uncle.

"Oh, my God," Shelley said, her voice trembling. "You saw Uncle Henry being killed." She nodded then, letting him know she understood. Claude looked relieved. "We have to let Captain Lasserre know," she said.

Shelley wanted to try to get Claude to stay at the house while she went to the village so Chantal could call the police. It was very important that Claude communicate what he knew.

She took him back to the solarium, signaling for him to stay. Then she went to the kitchen, and returned with water and something for him to eat. The poor fellow must have been starved because he stuffed the food in his mouth. Her heart went out to him as she watched him guzzle the glass of water.

When he'd wiped his mouth with his grimy sleeve and seemed content, Shelley tried to explain that she had to leave, but would be back shortly. Though he didn't seem to understand, he appeared to take comfort in her manner.

She was about to leave when an idea occurred to her. Taking the missing journal page from her purse, she showed it to Claude. He indicated recognition. Shelley pointed to the plants on the table, miming that she couldn't find it. He shook his head then, and pointed away.

"Show me where it is," she said, indicating what she meant by pointing to her eye, then at the drawing.

Claude nodded, took her by the arm and led her outside, around the house and down toward the road. Soon they were walking in the direction of the village. Shelley found this strange and thought that he had misunderstood.

They came to the bay where most of the villagers lived. Claude turned off the road and led her through the dense vegetation behind the houses. When they came to Chantal's, he crept to the edge of her back garden and pointed to a small greenhouse. Shelley understood him to mean the plant was inside.

Her pulse began racing as she considered the consequences. Had Chantal stolen the plant? Was she in the conspiracy against her uncle? Or was she innocent, like Jack?

In any case, she had to make sure that the plant was really there. Indicating for Claude to wait, she crept to the rear of the tiny greenhouse. Finding a clear pane of glass, she peered in. Sure enough, the exotic plant was there.

She was tremendously relieved to know that the plant hadn't fallen into Deitz-Langen's hands. Now all she had to do was take it and the drawing to Professor Dufour.

She led Claude back to the place where they'd left the road and gestured for him to wait. Then she went on into the village, heading back to Chantal's house. She was happy to find her home.

"*Tiens*," the Frenchwoman said, greeting her at the door. "Finally you come to visit me."

"Chantal, I can't explain now, but could you contact Captain Lasserre and have him come here as soon as he can?"

"Why? What's happened?"

"I think I know where Claude is. And I've discovered he has important evidence the police will be interested in."

Chantal frowned. "What sort of evidence?"

"Just call, Chantal. I'm not entirely sure myself."

"If you wish." Chantal beckoned her inside and went to the transmitter.

Shelley followed her. "Oh, and have him pass on a message to Professor Dufour. Have him tell the professor I've located the missing information."

"What missing information?"

"He'll understand."

Chantal made the call. The conversation was in French, but as best Shelley could tell, the proper message was passed along.

"Is he coming?" she asked when Chantal hung up.

"Yes. He was very happy about Claude. The person who can do sign is arriving this afternoon. Lasserre wishes to have them here for the interrogation. The professor might come along as well. They'll be here late in the afternoon."

"Good." Shelley headed for the door.

"You aren't leaving?" Chantal said.

"Yes, I need to get back to the plantation house. Maybe you could bring the police by when they arrive. It's the best place for us all to meet."

"If you wish." Chantal gave her a suspicious look. "You're sure everything is all right?"

"Yes," Shelley replied. "I'm sure."

She started to leave, but her curiosity made her hesitate. She'd been suspicious of Chantal ever since she'd learned how the woman had tried to cultivate Henry.

"You once said you knew nothing about my uncle's work, isn't that right?"

"Yes."

"Didn't he ever confide what he was doing, or share his research with you in any way?"

"No, never."

"But he told you he was expecting to receive some money."

"Yes, Shelley, but he didn't say from what source."

Not only was Shelley beginning to suspect Chantal was lying, but also that she was somehow involved in Henry's murder. She shuddered at the thought. "Well," she said, trying to sound cheerful, "I guess I'll see you this afternoon."

"You're sure you don't want to stay here?"

"No, thank you."

"Can I take you back in the Jeep?"

"No," Shelley answered. "I enjoy the walk."

"They say the people in California are married to their vehicles," Chantal remarked. "It isn't true for you?"

"The past few days have changed me a lot," Shelley replied. "More than you could possibly imagine."

CLAUDE WAS WAITING where she'd left him. It was a relief, because she'd had visions of him fleeing into the jungle, and taking the secret of Uncle Henry's murderer with him.

Claude trudged beside her like a friendly puppy. Shelley felt guilty for ever having been afraid of him, knowing that all he'd wanted was to convey the terrible secret he'd been holding. How hard it must have been for him to live with the knowledge that he'd seen his one friend killed.

When they got back to the plantation house, Shelley made Claude some lunch. He refused to come inside to eat, so she took it to the laboratory. Afterward, she brought him a chair and more blankets so that he could rest more comfortably. The first thing he did was take a nap.

Shelley waited on the veranda for Chantal and the police to arrive. The Frenchwoman would have some explaining to do, but Captain Lasserre could take care of that.

As the hours wore on, Shelley's thoughts returned again and again to Jack. She even flirted with the idea of abandoning her work to be with him, but she knew that wasn't right. Important as love was, it couldn't be a person's entire life. She needed her career, just as he needed his. And yet, the thought of leaving him, of leaving Saint Maurice, was terribly painful. It would be the most difficult goodbye of her life.

It had probably been a mistake to get involved, but Jack had been irresistible. And as long as she was on Saint Maurice, she'd be with him. That much she understood.

As she stared at the western sky, waiting for the plane to appear, Shelley realized she couldn't get Jack out of her mind. She missed him terribly. In fact, she was as anxious about him as she was about finding out who had murdered her uncle.

Late in the afternoon Shelley heard the sound of the Jeep, coming through the jungle.

Moments later it appeared, with Chantal driving, and Captain Lasserre beside her. In back were the young policeman who'd come last time, Professor Dufour, and a middle-aged woman, undoubtedly the sign interpreter. The vehicle came to a stop and Lasserre saluted her.

"Bonjour, madame," he said, stepping down from the Jeep and mounting the steps. "I understand you have captured our elusive witness and discovered important information."

"Stumbled on it would be more accurate, Captain Lasserre."

He glanced around. "And Monsieur Kincaid?"

"He hasn't returned yet. I expect him soon."

Lasserre introduced the sign interpreter to Shelley. Madame Blamont was stocky and broad-shouldered, with streaks of white in her black hair. They shook hands and Shelley led the group inside to the salon.

"Where is Claude Perrin?" Captain Lasserre asked when they were seated.

"He's in back," Shelley said. "I'll get him in a moment. But first I'd like to tell you what I've discovered." She was standing before them. Lasserre was in one easy chair, Professor Dufour in another. Chantal, Madame Blamont and the other gendarme were on the sofa.

Shelley got her purse from the side table, removed the missing journal page and handed it to Captain Lasserre. "I found this by chance at Jack's place this morning. This note was with it. I believe it explains his innocence in the matter."

Lasserre looked at the papers. *"Tiens!* It's the missing page from Monsieur Van Dam's notebook."

"Vraiment?" Philippe Dufour said excitedly. He got to his feet and went over to the captain's chair. "This is wonderful, *madame!*"

"It should enable you to carry out my uncle's wishes, Professor."

"I am so pleased," he said, beaming.

"There's more," Shelley continued. She took the page from Lasserre's hand and showed it to Chantal, who looked up at her with confusion. "Does this plant look familiar to you?"

Chantal studied the drawing. "Actually, it looks very much like a plant of Claude's that I am keeping in the greenhouse in my garden."

"Claude's?" Shelley echoed.

"Yes. A few months ago he brought it to me with a note from Henry saying that he'd brought this exotic plant back from his travels as a gift for Claude. He said there was a mold or fungus on some of the plants in his solarium and since this one was very delicate, he didn't want it to become diseased. He asked for me to keep it with my orchids until the fungus was under control."

"That's all? He didn't tell you the plant provided the key ingredient for the drug he'd discovered?"

"No. As I said, the note indicated the plant was Claude's. I thought nothing of it. Frankly, I forgot all about it until you showed me this paper."

Chantal seemed sincere—either that or she was very fast on her feet and an excellent actress. "Well," Shelley said, "that plant may be the key to the health of many thousands of people."

"Mon Dieu," Chantal exclaimed.

Shelley turned to Professor Dufour, who was looking positively joyous. She handed him the drawing. "Here's your missing ingredient, Professor."

"*Madame*, you are an angel!" Again he got to his feet and walked about excitedly, like a child who'd just opened a Christmas present.

"This is all very nice," Captain Lasserre said, "but what is the evidence you have? Do you know who murdered your uncle?"

"No, but we will soon find out. Madame Blamont, will you come with me for a second?" Shelley nodded politely to the others. "Please excuse us, we'll be right back."

She led the woman to the laboratory where they found Claude puttering with the orchids, a watering can in his hand. He acted a bit dismayed at the sight of a stranger.

"Tell him not to worry," she advised Madame Blamont. "Explain that we have something very important for him to do."

The woman signed, and Claude was overjoyed to finally be able to communicate with someone. Madame Blamont took a few moments to gain his confidence and explain that he would be accompanying them into the house to tell the police what he'd seen the day Henry was murdered.

The poor man was nervous and reluctant, but between Shelley and Madame Blamont he felt safe enough to go with them. Shelley led him into the salon. Claude was so shy that he hung his head and began wringing his hands.

Shelley addressed the chief gendarme. "Captain Lasserre, I believe Claude was outside the library window when my uncle was murdered. If I am right, he should be able to tell us who the culprit is."

"*Formidable!*" Lasserre cried, rising to his feet, his eyes wide with delight.

Shelley glanced at the others, all of whom looked absolutely mystified. She turned to Madame Blamont. "Will you have Claude tell us what happened, please."

The interpreter signed the question to Claude. He began his account and she translated as he signed.

"I went to my friend's house," she said. "I wished to see my orchid and give it water. As I passed by the window I saw my friend with another person. Their faces were very red and they were angry. I knew they were fighting...."

Madame Blamont's voice trailed off. Claude had stopped signing. He was looking across the room in the direction of Philippe Dufour. His mouth sagged open. He raised his arm and pointed to the professor with a shaking hand. Glancing at Madame Blamont, he signed again.

"It's him," she said with a quavering voice. "The man who killed my friend!"

The words were no sooner out of the woman's mouth than Claude began wheezing terribly. His face turned crimson and before anyone could stop him, he charged Philippe Dufour, his fists raised.

"Non, pas moi!" Dufour screamed as he raised his arms to fend off the blows. "Not me!"

The younger policeman quickly pulled Claude away from the professor and Lasserre rushed over to the terrified academician, who was straightening his glasses, his hands shaking.

"You must believe me," he wailed. "I didn't do it. Henry Van Dam was my friend. We had our disagreements," he stuttered, "but I certainly wouldn't hurt him.... Anything that happened was an accident—I mean, it wasn't my intention.... *Eh, mon Dieu!"*

Dufour sank into his chair, his head dropping into his hands. *"Non,"* he said, virtually weeping. "It wasn't me! It's all a terrible mistake."

Captain Lasserre glanced at Shelley, shaking his head sadly. She reached for the side table to steady herself as Philippe Dufour began to weep. "Good Lord," she mur-

mured, "he was Uncle Henry's friend, the one person in
the world he fully trusted." Amid the chaos around her,
Shelley thought of Jack. What she wouldn't have given just
then to hear his plane swoop overhead.

13

SHELLEY LEANED AGAINST one of the columns supporting the roof of the makeshift hangar. The light was fading fast. She hoped Jack hadn't been delayed so long that he would have to try to land in the dark.

She had come to the landing strip as soon as Chantal had driven the gendarmes and their prisoner away. But that had been over half an hour ago, and there hadn't been any sign of Jack's plane. Then Shelley heard the distant hum of an engine.

She turned to look in the direction of the approach and saw the Cessna in the distance, the last light of the sunset reflecting off its fuselage. She watched it draw near, holding her breath as it skimmed the treetops and settled onto the landing strip. She waved and moved to a safe spot until Jack had killed the engines.

When the plane came to a stop she ran around the wing and was practically bouncing up and down by the time the door opened and he descended into her arms. They kissed without saying a word. It was a frantic kiss, and she was reassured by the fact that he seemed every bit as happy to see her as she was to see him.

"God," he said, holding her close, "you've spoiled me for life. How am I ever going to be able to fly home again and not have you waiting for me?"

"I'm so glad to see you," she murmured, pressing her head to his chest.

He lifted her chin. "You're all I thought about today. I couldn't even keep my mind on my flying. Damned near landed at Saint Martin without putting my gear down."

"Oh, Jack..."

He put his arm around her shoulders and they started walking up the trail. "How was your day?" he asked.

"Eventful."

"Didn't have any trouble with Claude, did you? I worried about that."

"As a matter of fact, Claude and I caught Uncle Henry's killer. And I also found the missing page from the journal and the mystery plant that will save lives cheaply."

Jack stopped dead in his tracks. "Whoa, wait a minute." He looked at her in utter disbelief. "You caught the murderer?"

"Yes," she said, taking his hand.

As they walked on, Shelley told him the whole story.

"I can't believe it," he said when she described how Claude had attacked Philippe Dufour and the professor had broken down. "I thought he was in France at the time of the murder."

"That's what everybody assumed. But he confessed everything. According to what Captain Lasserre told me, Deitz-Langen had enlisted the professor's support in convincing Uncle Henry to sell his discovery to them. They chartered a boat and sent Philippe here a month ago just for that purpose. He was determined to be discreet about it and wanted to catch Uncle Henry off guard and unprepared.

"When Uncle Henry realized that Philippe was in league with the Germans, he became enraged. They argued, and in a fit of anger the professor picked up the chessboard and struck Uncle Henry. Realizing what he'd done, he dragged the body to the foot of the stairs and tried to make it look like an accident, just as we'd suspected.

"Philippe intended to tell the authorities that he'd found Henry dead when he arrived, but then he realized nobody except the people on the charter boat knew he'd even been there. So he returned to France, hoping his presence wouldn't be discovered. He told everyone at Deitz-Langen that Uncle Henry had refused the offer.

"The notes Uncle Henry wrote to me and Monsieur Voirin were written long before he discovered the professor had betrayed him. And of course, Henry was killed before he could warn anyone."

"So Dufour decided to lay low," Jack guessed. "And when you contacted him, saying you wanted him to have control of the research, he must have felt like he was living a charmed life."

"Yes, he was going to get the profits of his evil deed handed to him on a silver platter. Before that, he knew nothing about Uncle Henry's plan to put him in charge."

"Who was behind the burglary? Dufour?"

"No, he knew nothing about that. He hadn't been in contact with Deitz-Langen after informing them of his failed mission. But Captain Lasserre believes that when the company learned that Uncle Henry was dead, they decided to get the critical research before somebody else did. The same German agency chartered boats from Saint Martin both at the time of the murder and at the time of the burglary. In both cases the principal was Deitz-Langen. Karl Baumann is being questioned now and they feel that either he or someone else at Deitz-Langen was behind the burglary."

"Not realizing that it was all going to fall into the hands of their friend Philippe Dufour," Jack continued.

"That's right. They, like everybody else, thought Uncle Henry had died in an accident. If it hadn't been for Claude, the professor probably would have gotten away with it, and then would have made a fortune by selling out to Deitz-Langen."

The plantation house was in view, but Shelley hardly gave it a glance. Pulling on Jack's hand, she was eager to get home to his place.

"So what happens to Henry's discovery now?" Jack asked.

"It's up to us to see that the drug is developed and marketed according to my uncle's wishes."

"*Us?*"

"If you're going to receive twenty-five percent of the profits, you ought to earn it."

"I don't want that money, Shelley. You can have it all."

"You've got a responsibility, Jack. Uncle Henry wanted you involved for a reason."

"Much as I loved the old boy," he told her, "what he wanted doesn't concern me. It's what you want that matters."

"I want you to help me with this," she said. "I really do."

He fell silent then, until they reached his cottage. He went right out to the terrace and stood there with his hands on his hips, watching the fading color in the western sky.

Shelley stood behind him, staring at his shadowed silhouette. He was obviously unhappy with what she'd said. She'd been too pushy, she decided. Going to his side, she put her arm around his waist and said, "I'm sorry I put pressure on you, Jack. That isn't fair. You didn't ask for any of this—even holding my hand these past few days. Uncle Henry sort of crammed me down your throat."

He pulled her tightly against him. "It was the best thing Henry ever did."

"How can it be good to bring two people together who belong in two different worlds?"

"You wouldn't stay here on Saint Maurice with me, if I asked you?"

"I'd love to be with you, Jack, but how long would it last? We can't live on love and dreams."

"I suppose you're right."

"You wouldn't want to come and live with me in L.A., would you?"

"No."

"You see?"

Jack held her head against him and kissed the top of it. Again he reflected, staring out at the sea. "What would it take to entice you to move here?" he finally asked.

"I suppose if I brought my office and all my charities here, I could do it. I could get by without putting in a freeway but I'd need the people I work for and with."

"You don't need all that stuff. What's really essential? A telephone? A computer with a modem? A fax machine?"

"Jack, this place doesn't even have electricity. Hot water is a luxury. And you want me to run a business from here?"

"We're going to be rich. We'll put in electricity. We'll fix up the plantation house. We'll pave the road and improve the airport so that your lawyers and accountants and clients can all come and see you."

"You must want me around pretty badly to pave over paradise."

He took her by the shoulders. "Shelley, I've spent the whole day trying to figure out how to keep you here on a permanent basis. Having a paved road and electricity for a microwave oven and a VCR will not destroy my life."

"Why the compromise? So you'll have a girl in the home port?"

He tweaked her nose. "Not a girl . . . A . . ." He looked into her eyes and she waited. "You're going to make me say the *M* word, aren't you?"

"Jack, I've fallen in love with you, but that doesn't mean a thing this early. You know that as well as I do."

"So take a week or two to see how you feel."

She laughed.

"Don't keep me hanging, Shelley. I really want to know you aren't going to leave."

"You're serious about this, aren't you?"

"Damned right, I am."

"Serious enough that you'd be willing to fly around Southern California for six months out of every year in exchange for me working from here during the other six months?"

Jack rubbed his chin contemplatively. "Six months, huh?"

"Seems fair to me. Fifty-fifty compromise. Right down the middle."

Jack pointed out at the sea, lying tranquilly like a vast pool of ink under the evening sky. "After dinner we're going to take the ketch out there. Then, in the moonlight, we're going to negotiate this thing."

"You call that a negotiation?"

"What do you call it?"

"Unfair," she said.

"What do you suggest we do to resolve this?"

"I propose that we play a game of chess. If I win, it's six months each place."

"And what if I win?"

She cuffed him playfully on the chin. "Then we go out on your boat and negotiate."

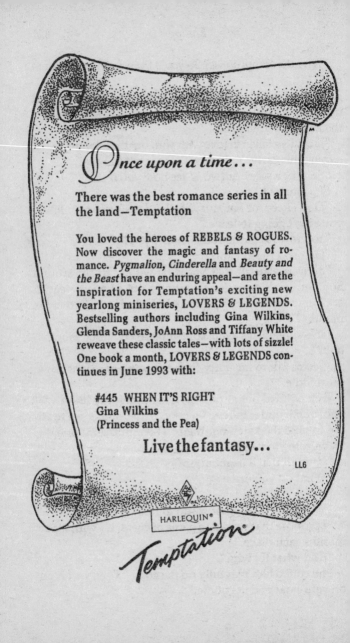

Once upon a time...

There was the best romance series in all the land—Temptation

You loved the heroes of REBELS & ROGUES. Now discover the magic and fantasy of romance. *Pygmalion, Cinderella* and *Beauty and the Beast* have an enduring appeal—and are the inspiration for Temptation's exciting new yearlong miniseries, LOVERS & LEGENDS. Bestselling authors including Gina Wilkins, Glenda Sanders, JoAnn Ross and Tiffany White reweave these classic tales—with lots of sizzle! One book a month, LOVERS & LEGENDS continues in June 1993 with:

#445 WHEN IT'S RIGHT
Gina Wilkins
(Princess and the Pea)

Live the fantasy...

LL6

HARLEQUIN®

Temptation

THREE UNFORGETTABLE HEROINES
THREE AWARD-WINNING AUTHORS

Untamed

MAVERICK HEARTS

A unique collection of historical short stories that capture the spirit of America's last frontier.

HEATHER GRAHAM POZZESSERE—over 10 million copies of her books in print worldwide
Lonesome Rider—The story of an Eastern widow and the renegade half-breed who becomes her protector.

PATRICIA POTTER—an author whose books are consistently Waldenbooks bestsellers
Against the Wind—Two people, battered by heartache, prove that love can heal all.

JOAN JOHNSTON—award-winning Western historical author with 17 books to her credit
One Simple Wish—A woman with a past discovers that dreams really do come true.

Join us for an exciting journey West with
UNTAMED
Available in July, wherever Harlequin books are sold.

MAV93

Fifty red-blooded, white-hot, true-blue hunks from every State in the Union!

Beginning in May, look for MEN MADE IN AMERICA! Written by some of our most popular authors, these stories feature fifty of the strongest, sexiest men, each from a different state in the union!

Two titles available every other month at your favorite retail outlet.

In May, look for:

FULL HOUSE by Jackie Weger (Alabama)
BORROWED DREAMS by Debbie Macomber (Alaska)

In July, look for:

CALL IT DESTINY by Jayne Ann Krentz (Arizona)
ANOTHER KIND OF LOVE by Mary Lynn Baxter (Arkansas)

You won't be able to resist MEN MADE IN AMERICA!

MEN593